"Deputy," he said, giving her a polite nod.

"Snake handler," she replied, her voice even, though her eyes glowed with banked fury.

He chuckled, mentally tallying up a point in her favor. "Just doin' my job, ma'am," he answered, giving her a tip of an invisible hat.

Peeking around the corner of the building, he spotted a sliver of shade he might claim for himself. He was about to wind his way through the waiting customers when he heard her mutter, "Whatever helps you sleep at night."

"I sleep the sleep of the innocent, Deputy Cabrera," he said, meeting her gaze. "Every night I indulge in the peaceful, unfettered rest of a man with a clear conscience."

"You're certainly no Wendell Wingate," she retorted, not backing down an inch.

He shook his head at her reference to his grandfather. "Ah, I hate to tell you this, but you're wrong."

FOR THE DEFENSE

—

MAGGIE WELLS

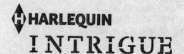

HARLEQUIN

INTRIGUE

For Bill, my sweet-talking Southern man. We're two decades
into this fling and you still make my heart sing.

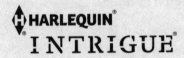

Recycling programs
for this product may
not exist in your area.

ISBN-13: 978-1-335-48910-4

For the Defense

Copyright © 2021 by Margaret Ethridge

This edition published by arrangement with Harlequin Books S.A.

For questions and comments about the quality of this book,
please contact us at CustomerService@Harlequin.com.

Harlequin Enterprises ULC
22 Adelaide St. West, 40th Floor
Toronto, Ontario M5H 4E3, Canada
www.Harlequin.com

Printed in U.S.A.

By day **Maggie Wells** is buried in spreadsheets. At night she pens tales of intrigue and people tangling up the sheets. She has a weakness for hot heroes and happy endings. She is the product of a charming rogue and a shameless flirt, and you only have to scratch the surface of this mild-mannered married lady to find a naughty streak a mile wide.

Books by Maggie Wells

Harlequin Intrigue

A Raising the Bar Brief

An Absence of Motive
For the Defense

Visit the Author Profile page at Harlequin.com.

CAST OF CHARACTERS

Lourdes (Lori) Cabrera—Lori is proud of her small-town roots and of her job as a Masters County sheriff's deputy, but she's certain Samuel Coulter's Reptile Refuge is something more sinister than a tourist trap.

Simon Wingate—The scion of a family entrenched in Georgia politics who stumbles each time he tries to stand out. His biggest client to date is a multimillionaire who also happens to be an exotic-snake enthusiast...among other things.

Samuel Coulter—An eccentric millionaire from South Florida who bought a large parcel of property in Masters County and has built his own reptile refuge. The problem is, he may be dealing in more than exotic snakes.

Ben Kinsella—Former DEA agent turned rural county sheriff.

Harrison Hayes—The district attorney for Masters County.

Alicia Simmons—One of Ben's friends from the DEA, she has come to town on a mission to bring Coulter down.

Wendell Wingate—Simon's grandfather. He built the Masters County law firm Simon is running, and now he's campaigning for a seat on the circuit court bench.

Chapter One

"Interview with Deputy Lourdes Cabrera, Masters County Sheriff's Department. Deputy Cabrera, would you please tell us what you witnessed in the early-morning hours of September 28?"

Lori had to refrain from rolling her eyes while Danielle Anderson spoke into her cell like it was a microphone. She understood the need for an official statement, but the assistant district attorney sounded like she was reading from a television script. They may not have been besties, but they worked in separate wings of the same building. Heck, they'd been at the same Chic Chef housewares party the previous weekend. But for the sake of the teenage girl she'd picked up walking Highway 19 alone at two in the morning, Lori tamped down the urge to snark and spoke directly into the microphone on the proffered device.

"I was returning from a call when I saw a young girl—uh, a female who appeared to be underage— walking along the side of the road."

"You'd had a call so late?" Danielle interrupted.

This time, Lori did smirk, and she shot a look at the sheriff seated at his desk at the back of the room. Sheriff Ben Kinsella wore a bemused half smile. They complained all the time about how civilians didn't actually understand their jobs, and their own assistant district attorney had proved them right. Calls in the wee hours were not at all out of the ordinary in their line of work, even in small rural communities.

"Yes. There'd been a report of a domestic disturbance at a home on Highway 19 west of the county line. I took the call through direct dispatch. I was already out on patrol and requested backup from Prescott County since many of the lots in the area straddle the county line. We often provide backup for one another in those situations," she explained.

"You were heading back toward Pine Bluff when you noticed the young woman walking alone so late?"

"Yes." Lori shifted closer to the edge of the chair.

"Can you tell me what made you stop?"

Lori blinked. Sometimes she forgot not everyone would have pulled over for a stranger walking along the road at such a dangerous hour. Cop or not. "I stopped because it's dangerous for people to walk along unlit county roads in the dark of night," she replied evenly.

"The person you picked up, was she known to you?"

Lori had to force herself to remember they were having this pedantic discussion for a reason. Leaning closer to the phone, she looked up at the ADA and spoke directly into the phone. "No, ma'am. I had never met her." She moved back, carefully maintaining eye contact with the lawyer. "I pulled to the side of the road and approached her from behind, identifying myself as a sheriff's deputy."

"Did she try to run?"

The question made Lori frown. "No." She paused, trying to figure out the attorney's angle. "Well, I guess technically she did, but she ran toward me," she said, enunciating each word for the sake of eventual transcription.

"She ran toward you and said what?" Danielle prompted.

"She said, 'Thank God. Can you help me? I want to go home.'" A shiver raced down Lori's spine when she recalled the edgy desperation in the girl's voice.

"What happened then?"

"I took her name and address. Bella Nunes. She gave me a street address in Jennings, Florida. When I found her, she was dressed in a pair of bathing suit bottoms, a tank top and a pair of cheap rubber flip-flops. No purse, no ID."

She stopped there, thinking back over the information she'd been able to glean from the trembling girl between sobs.

"She told me she was fifteen. She said she'd been staying with a friend who moved up here, but that she wanted to go home. When I pressed her about the friend's identity, she clammed up."

"Ms. Nunes offered no other information? Where this friend lived? A name?"

Lori shook her head. "No. She refused to tell me where she was coming from or who she'd been with."

"Did you have some suspicions based on where she'd been walking and knowledge of the residents in the area?" Danielle probed.

Lori glanced over at her boss, needing the reassurance she hadn't gone off half-cocked when drawing her conclusions. The sheriff inclined his head, urging her to continue.

"There are only three residences within a two-mile radius of where I found Ms. Nunes. I didn't see her on my way out there, and when I found her, she wasn't walking at a brisk pace. One of the straps on her sandals had broken. The edges of the road are crumbling. She told me she was scared to walk in the grass because of snakes."

"Snakes?"

"Said she'd seen enough snakes to last a lifetime," Lori answered flatly.

"And she wouldn't say where she was coming from?" Danielle repeated.

"No." Lori leaned forward, her gaze locked on the other woman as she spoke. "There are only three residences in the radius. One was the residence I was called to for the domestic disturbance. One is owned by a widow named Hazel Johnson and is located closer to town. When we passed, I checked, and all of the lights at Mrs. Johnson's place were out."

"And the property belonging to Samuel Coulter was the only one left?" Danielle asked.

"Yes."

"What type of business does Mr. Coulter run on his property?"

Lori was about to answer when the door to the sheriff's department swung open and the district attorney, Harrison Hayes, strode in. "Hold up," he said, lifting a hand to back up his order.

Danielle jabbed at the screen to stop the recording. The familiar squeak and roll of Ben's desk chair told her the sheriff had come to his feet. The grim resignation on the DA's face made a knot of ice form in her stomach. Obviously, the DA's meeting with Samuel Coulter and his attorney hadn't gone as expected.

Rising to her feet, Lori peered through the floor-to-ceiling glass walls into the reception area separating the county's legal offices from the law enforcement branch. She spotted them by the empty mosaic-tiled fountain. Two men, one nearly as handsome as the other, but both equally repugnant to her.

Coulter and his attorney, Simon Wingate, stood with their heads bent close to one another. Lori's lip curled. There'd been few sightings of the eccentric millionaire since he'd bought the massive acreage out on Highway 19. She'd heard rumors about the man being good-looking, but... Lori narrowed her eyes. He wasn't just handsome; he was gorgeous.

Disgusted with the thought, she shifted her attention to the man's clothes. What did a man suspected of endangering young women wear to be questioned by the local prosecutors? Loose linen pants and a finely woven white shirt. And flip-flops. Not the cheap dollar-store shower shoes Bella'd been wearing. No, his had wide straps fashioned from supple leather. He looked like a guy on vacation.

The sandals were a sharp contrast to the impeccably shined wing tips the man standing next to him wore.

Simon Wingate looked every inch the prep-school-educated politician's son.

Lori clenched her back teeth and focused on the man in the expertly tailored suit. He was the light to his client's dark. The perfect foil. All warm, gold-tipped curls, crinkly blue eyes and sun-kissed skin. Lori was woman enough to admit her mouth sometimes watered when she saw Simon Wingate. Not today, though.

Masters County's newest resident had lawyered up and come to head them off at the pass. No doubt Coulter waved a wad of cash, and city slicker Simon had come a-runnin'. Judging by Coulter's unperturbed expression and the district attorney's abrupt halt to Lori's statement, whatever they said had worked. He was about to slither out the doors of Masters County Municipal Center a free man.

"Snakes," Lori said, her gaze following the two men exiting the building. The outer door closed behind them, and she refocused her indignation on the DA. "The man buys, sells and breeds exotic snakes."

"Which is not illegal," Hayes replied calmly.

"Bella Nunes said he threatened her with his damn snakes," Lori blurted, losing her cool at last.

Hayes held up a placating hand. "I am aware of Ms. Nunes's accusations. I am also aware she is not fifteen. She is actually eighteen years old, a three-time runaway prior to her eighteenth birthday, and has a history of embellishing stories when she gets caught in a difficult spot. Or so her parents say."

Sheriff Kinsella approached. "You're not pressing charges?"

Hayes shrugged. "Would if I thought I could get something to stick. All I have is a complaint filed by a young woman who claimed to be fifteen, when in fact she is eighteen. She is an adult who admits she came here of her own free will, whether she regrets that decision now or not. She said herself no one was around when Coulter allegedly—"

Offended on Bella's behalf, Lori bristled. "He locked her in a cage with a boa constrictor!"

"So she says," the district attorney retorted, his expression grave. "He says he didn't and has offered to provide witnesses to refute Ms. Nunes's claims. She has no witnesses to say she was mistreated. Our hands are tied."

The man's mouth flattened into a grim line, and Lori could see he didn't care for the outcome of his interview with Coulter any more than she did. Exhaling with a whoosh, she dropped back into her chair and made a concerted effort not to appear sulky.

"Right. I get you," she conceded.

The prosecutor inclined his head, the corners of his mouth pulled tight. "Mr. Coulter has generously offered to pay for her bus ticket back to Florida."

"What a guy." Danielle pocketed her phone and headed for the door.

The rhetorical statement caused the sheriff to snort. Harrison Hayes's expression, on the other hand, remained somber while he watched his associate approach.

At last, the DA cracked. A smirk twisting his lips, he held the lobby door open for Danielle. After making sure the door was closed again, he pivoted, a hand raised in helpless surrender. "For what it's worth, I don't disagree with your instincts, Deputy. There is something off about the guy, and I'm not only talking about the snake eyes."

"Snake eyes?" Ben asked.

"So he does have creepy eyes?" Lori asked, swiping Bella Nunes's choice of descriptors.

Hayes gestured to his own left eye. "Elongated pupil," he explained. "I'm man enough to admit it's disconcerting, given the guy's obsession with reptiles."

Lori nodded, her lips quirking at Hayes's barely concealed shudder. "You think he's some sort of cult leader?"

"He may be, but I can tell you this," the DA said, opening the office door again. "I wouldn't follow the guy across the street."

When they were gone, Lori swiveled her chair to face her boss. "Well, damn."

Ben nodded and moved back to his own desk. "She's spent the morning at Reverend Mitchell's house. I'll go by and let them know what's happening. I'm sure I can work something out with him on the bus ticket. Maybe there's some kind of charity fund.

If not, I'll talk to Marlee. I don't want Ms. Nunes to feel beholden to Coulter in any way."

Lori hid her smile. When Ben's girlfriend, Marlee Masters, had come home to Pine Bluff, most of the townspeople had been poised to write her off as nothing more than the small-town princess she'd been once upon a time—pretty and petted and cooed over by everyone. Marlee had changed since the loss of her only brother. Her father had suffered a debilitating stroke a few months prior, and Marlee had not only taken over the reins of the family business, but she'd also stepped straight into the role of civic leader.

Marlee was a Masters of Masters County, Georgia. If she wanted there to be a charity doling out bus tickets home to wayward young women with questionable taste in men, by God, there'd be one set up by morning.

"Thank you." Lori sighed and closed the spiral notebook she had open on the desk. She'd had her notes all ready in case she needed to refer to them while making her statement, but she might as well ball them up and toss them in the trash.

"We'll maintain a closer watch on things happening out along Highway 19," Ben said, keeping the order casual and open. "Tourists have started coming to visit Cottonmouth Coulter's Reptile Rendezvous. From what I hear, it's all the kids in town can talk about. We should be on guard for an uptick in activity."

Lori bit her lip. She knew she was too personally invested in Bella Nunes's drama. She used to be bet-

ter at compartmentalizing stuff like this, but lately…
Lately Lori was having a harder time keeping a tight
lid on her emotions. She sensed Ben was aware of
her struggle, was throwing her a bone. Lori appreciated his concern but at the same time wished she
could just suck it up.

Thankfully, Ben believed in her hunch about Coulter. They were experienced, intuitive cops who put
stock in niggling suspicion. Suspicion often turned
into hard evidence. They were both the sorts who
weren't afraid to pick and pull at the flimsiest of
threads to see what unraveled and what they could
learn from the results.

"I'll talk to Mike about it when he comes on shift.
Give him some pointers on what to look out for."
She dropped her notes on the Nunes incident into
the shredder near the desk she shared with Deputy
Mike Schaeffer.

Mike's seniority irked her. He'd only been at the
sheriff's department two weeks longer than her and
had less experience. She'd finished her initial entry
training at Fort Leonard Wood and stayed on for military police school. She finished her stint in the cor-
rections brigade at Fort Leavenworth, Kansas. Mike,
a homegrown boy who'd graduated a year behind her,
had partied at the University of Georgia for a couple
of semesters. After he failed to make the grade there,
he landed at Georgia Piedmont Tech's law enforcement academy, and he was hired two weeks after his
twenty-first birthday.

Loyal and almost too eager to please, Mike was

a nice guy. Which made it even harder for her to re-sent him. Most of the time. Though it irked her that she seemed destined to train men who outranked her.

"How about a milkshake?" Ben asked, jolting her from her thoughts. "I sure could use something cold and sweet to wash this sour taste out of my mouth."

Lori saw him wriggling his wallet from his back pocket. "You buying?"

"I'll buy if you fly," he offered.

"Done." She pushed back from the desk, thankful to have an excuse to go for a walk. The Daisy Drive-In was only a few blocks away. Maybe a short walk and a tall shake were exactly what she needed.

Outside the stagnant office, the day was warm, though the calendar claimed it was still September. In South Georgia, autumn didn't come around until late October. Tipping her chin up, she tugged at the front of her uniform shirt in hopes of wafting cool air over her superheated skin. She took two deep breaths and reminded herself it was okay to feel shaken, as long as she didn't let setbacks knock her down. Or so a therapist had once told her.

Unclenching her fists, she set off for the drive-in, but no matter how fast she walked, she couldn't out-pace her frustration. She couldn't believe they would let Coulter go without a reprimand. It galled her to think of the slime bag luring young women to his "refuge," tormenting them into thinking he was doing them a favor by letting them stay there.

As if she'd summoned the devil by thinking of him, an engine roared and a sports car shot past her. She caught sight of Coulter's tanned skin and dark, wind-tousled hair. *Of course he drives a Viper*, she thought with a sneer. What a cliché. Reflective sunglasses glinted in the sunlight, and her stomach flipped when he lifted a hand in a mocking wave and punched the gas.

He sped out of town at about thirty over the posted speed limit.

She pressed the button on the mic she wore clipped to her shoulder and tipped her head to the side, watching the car shrink into a pinprick in the distance. "Mike? What's your twenty?"

There was a crackle of static. Then the deputy on patrol answered. "I'm on Sawtooth Lake Road near the county line. Over."

Scowling, she peered at the strip of highway leading from the center of Pine Bluff toward the eastern half of Masters County. Mike was somewhere in the northwest quadrant. There'd be no catching Coulter today.

"Didja need me?" Mike asked, breaking into her thoughts.

She shook her head and keyed the mic. "Nope. False alarm. Carry on."

"Ten-four," Mike responded. "See you back at base."

They'd catch up to Coulter one day. They'd figure out exactly what he had going on and they'd stop it. They had to. Something bad was happening out there. She felt it in her bones.

Lori straightened her shoulders and refocused on the sight of the Daisy Drive-In in the distance. Today might not have been the day, but it was coming. Soon. She only hoped it would be soon enough to help the next young woman they found wandering the side of a rural highway in the dead of night.

Chapter Two

Simon Wingate kept the smile he wore plastered to his face until the client he'd waved off was nothing but a distant roar heading down the highway leading out of town. As he spun toward the converted Victorian that housed his grandfather's—now his—law offices, a shudder ran through him. If his grandfather were here, he'd have been able to get the old man's opinion on his new client. But his grandfather spent most of his time in Valdosta these days, having decided to run for a seat on the circuit court bench.

And Simon was here in Pine Bluff—also known as purgatory.

He missed Atlanta. What he wouldn't give for an evening spent talking strategy with his clients in restaurants with cloth napkins or sampling single malts with his fellow lobbyists at a whiskey bar. He never thought he'd come to appreciate what he'd once considered froufrou food, but when the only dining options in town were a bakery, a diner and a drive-in specializing in burgers and onion rings, even a man's man started dreaming of non-deep-fried food.

His stomach growled as he stared at the front door of the stately old home his grandfather had converted into law offices. He wasn't ready to go back in there. He wasn't in the mood to answer his secretary's questions or entertain her commentary on how his grandfather would have handled things. He was all too aware this was his grandfather's town. And Simon couldn't shake the niggling suspicion he'd never be able to fill Wendell Wingate's shoes.

Pivoting on the heel of his cap-toe oxford, he walked away from the office. He'd go to the drive-in and get something to eat. Then he'd come back and listen to Dora's litany of all he'd done wrong that morning.

He hadn't gone more than a half block before he felt his shirt adhere to his back. An hour earlier, the charcoal suit with the windowpane pattern seemed the perfect choice to represent a client at the DA's office. Now he was sorry he'd wasted the fine tailoring on a man who believed flip-flops were acceptable footwear anywhere not covered in sand.

He paused at the corner of Red Pine and Loblolly and looked back. The old courthouse planted in the center of the town square gleamed white in the late-morning sun. It had long ago been converted into a museum and home to the historical society, but a part of him wished they heard cases in the gracious old building rather than in the bland municipal complex.

He hooked a right on Pond Street, and the canopies of the Daisy Drive-In came into view. His steps faltered, but his stomach growled again. He pressed a hand to his abdomen to quell the uprising. He'd eaten at the dairy bar far too many times since he'd come back to town. So many times, in fact, that he'd started jogging. Outdoors. In the South Georgia heat. Because there were no gyms in this godforsaken—

"Morning, Simon," a cheerful voice called.

Jolted from his snit-fit, he whipped his head around to see Reverend Mitchell coming down the walkway in front of a small brick home. "Good morning, Reverend," he said, mustering his smile once more. Thankfully, he didn't feel the need to woo the clergyman the way he would a client, so he didn't amp up the wattage. Nodding toward the brick house, he asked, "Is this your place?"

The older man chuckled. "My lawn is not particularly well-kept. This is Maisy Tillenger's house. She's been under the weather, so Luellen and I have been checking in on her. Since we had company this morning, Luellen sent me."

Simon was aware the sheriff's department had taken the young woman who accused Coulter of mistreating her to the pastor's house. He let the comment about company slide by without remark. "Kind of you."

Good thing the reverend was a discreet man himself. "All part of the service," he replied jovially. He pointed to a shiny Buick parked at the curb. "You headin' for the Daisy? I could give you a lift."

Simon hesitated. Though he enjoyed the same easy country manners employed by his grandfather, he couldn't help being suspicious of the small-town bonhomie exhibited by so many of Pine Bluff's residents. He was a city guy. The son of a politician to boot. He firmly believed the world was fueled by quid pro quo. Perhaps the preacher wanted to score some free legal advice? Man of the cloth or not, he'd hardly be the first person who tried to wriggle around paying billable hours by engaging in some friendly conversation.

"I appreciate the offer, but if it's all the same to you, I think I'll walk. I've got some stuff I'm thinking through."

Reverend Mitchell didn't seem fazed by the refusal. "I understand." Rather than moving toward his car, the man stepped directly into Simon's path. "If you need a sounding board for anything you're noodling, you can always come to me. Again, all part of the service."

He smiled, and Simon was struck by the other man's innate ease and warmth. Regret twisted in his chest. He hated being so jaded. He didn't want to believe he was the kind of man who read something into everything. Then again, he'd learned at the foot of the master. A lifelong politician, his own father was the king of wheeling and dealing. From birth, Simon had been groomed to enter the arena.

"Thank you, sir," Simon said evenly. "Enjoy your day."

"You too, son," the reverend replied, clapping him on the shoulder. "Might I suggest you ask Miss Darlene to add extra cherries to your co-cola? There's no better pick-me-up for a bad day."

Simon's jaw slackened when the older man slid behind the wheel, slick as an eel. "How do you—"

The *ka-thunk* of the car door cut off the question. Reverend Mitchell cranked the engine and lifted two fingers from the wheel in farewell and pulled away from the curb.

"Friggin' fishbowl," he muttered. Stepping over a hump where a tree root had broken through the sidewalk, he resisted the urge to kick the loose pebbles skidding beneath the soles of his shoes because rocks and fine Italian leather rarely mixed well.

In a concession to the warmth of the day, he unbuttoned his suit jacket and loosened the silk tie enough to open his collar button. A fine coating of perspiration slicked his forehead and made the thin white cotton of his undershirt cling. Undaunted, he pressed on.

The grumble and pop of a souped-up engine brought him up short when he reached the cracked asphalt of the Daisy Drive-In's parking lot. A dinged-up subcompact with a ridiculous-looking spoiler rolled right past him, not bothering to yield to his right of way. Simon glared at the driver. The kid's arms were covered in mixture of amateur and professional tattoos. He was wearing a dirty ribbed undershirt and a trucker's cap with the bill turned to the side. Like he was some kind of backwoods hip-hop star. The worst of it was he had the gall to sneer when he gave Simon the once-over as he crept past.

The engine popped and roared, drawing the attention of nearly everyone waiting in line. The rear end fishtailed when the kid punched the accelerator and zipped toward the highway. Customers shook their heads as they stood in line at the order window. Simon approached, winding his way through the clumps of people chatting as they waited for their orders. No one greeted him, though he was sure they knew who he was. Or rather, who his grandfather was.

He nodded to a couple of men about his age. He hadn't been back in town long enough to renew the few acquaintances he'd made when his parents used to insist he spend his summers at his grandparents' house. Of course, he'd revisited here and there. Mainly quick swings through town when his father, a state assemblyman, was up for reelection.

He'd been studying abroad when his grandmother passed nearly ten years earlier. Both his father and grandfather insisted the trip home from Tokyo would require too much time off from his program. The people of Grandpa Wendell's beloved town hadn't understood or cared about their reasoning. Unlike the shameless flirts and meddling matchmakers he ran into in Atlanta, the over-sixty set in Pine Bluff had little use for him. He could swear he'd seen one or two of them steer their precious granddaughters away from him if they happened to pass in the Piggly Wiggly. Most settled for giving him the hairy eyeball.

Simon jerked to a stop two feet behind the last person in line. A woman turned to glare at him, but he tried not to take it personally. Brushing the sides of his suit coat back to allow some air to flow around his heated body, he lifted his gaze to meet hers and she quickly looked away. The woman turned away and he realized there was something familiar about her. She was young. And obviously not a fan.

Simon searched his memory, sure he'd have remembered her if they'd been introduced. Shifting from one foot to the other, he tried to get a better look. She wore her rich, dark hair pulled ruthlessly back from her face and coiled into a massive bun at the nape of her neck. The effect should have been severe, but for some reason, it intrigued him. He wanted to pull the pins from the knot and let the heavy locks down. He wanted to see how far down her back they flowed.

The line moved forward, and when they settled into their new formation, he saw the woman stepping up to the window. She wore a tan-and-brown uniform with a patch sewed onto the shirtsleeve that declared the wearer to be a member of the Masters County Sheriff's Department. Simon grimaced when he realized this was probably the deputy who'd taken the statement given against his client. Simon wasn't dumb enough to think he'd be high on the sheriff's office's list of favorite people after helping Samuel Coulter wriggle off the hook. Judging by the scornful look in her eyes, he wasn't wrong.

Simon stood frozen in place, watching her bend low to speak through the screen window. She must have a standing order, because with a minimum of words exchanged, the woman walked away clutching the tiny white slip with her order number printed on it.

Simon wanted to step out of line and directly into

her path as she moved to join the people milling and lounging near the pickup window. Explain that he'd only been doing the job he'd been hired to do, and that truthfully, Coulter gave him the creeps too. She wouldn't believe him even if he told her. Her glare made her disdain clear.

When his grandfather had droned on and on about how providing defense from the law was truly one of the most honorable things a man could do, Simon had only listened with half an ear. He'd been surrounded by and immersed in politics for too long to truly believe most people were innocent until proved guilty. In his experience, most people were guilty as sin when it came to being self-serving. Including himself. Look where that had landed him…in Pine Bluff.

Coulter certainly had his own best interests at heart. When Dora Houseman, the secretary he'd inherited along with his grandfather's firm, informed him the man's nickname was Cottonmouth, Simon had assumed it was because he was in the business of importing, breeding and selling exotic snakes at the multiacre refuge he'd set up on the other side of the county. In meeting him, Simon had to admit Coulter had likely earned his nickname based on his slithery personality. And his weird eyes.

The man's left pupil bled down to the bottom of his iris. The anomaly alone wasn't what made his stare so disturbing. A flat ruthlessness shone from his gold-green gaze. Simon himself had avoided looking directly at Coulter for any protracted amount of time.

Shaking off his discomfiture, Simon stepped to

the order window when the woman ahead of him moved aside.

"Heya, Mr. Simon," the gum-smacking older woman called Darlene greeted him, her grin bordering on a leer. "Cherry Coke?"

Her presumptive friendliness rankled, but he refused to let it show. Any misstep he made in this town would be reported to his grandfather within hours, no doubt. "Yes, please," he confirmed with the distant smile he'd perfected when he was a child trotted out at campaign events. "And today I'll try the club sandwich."

Darlene whooped and scrawled the order on her pad. "Mr. Simon Wingate is finally ready to join the mile-high club," she crowed. She ripped the claim check from the bottom of the order slip and slid it across the counter. She tapped it twice with the pointed tip of one bloodred acrylic nail. "I'm the woman to make it happen for ya, sugar."

The woman working the grill cackled. The young lady working the milkshake station ducked her head and murmured a mortified "Mama!"

Darlene smiled up at him, unrepentant. "I'll give a shout when it's ready, darlin'."

Simon could feel the heat in his cheeks and ears, and hoped anyone looking might attribute his blush to the temperature and layers of clothing. He moved from the window, hoping to find a shady spot along the side of the building far away from Darlene to wait, but found himself face-to-face with the woman with the tightly coiled hair. Lourdes Cabrera. She of the soulful eyes and Masters County Sheriff's Department uniform. He didn't have to check her name tag to be sure. The hostility in her stance said it all.

"Deputy," he said, giving her a polite nod.

"Snake handler," she replied, keeping her voice even, though her eyes glowed with banked fury.

He chuckled, mentally tallying up a point in her favor. "Just doin' my job, ma'am," he answered, giving her a tip of an invisible hat.

Peeking around the corner of the building, he spotted a sliver of shade he might claim for himself. He was about to wind his way through the waiting customers when he heard her mutter, "Whatever helps you sleep at night."

"I sleep the sleep of the innocent, Deputy Cabrera," he said, meeting her gaze. "Every night I indulge in the peaceful, unfettered rest of a man with a clear conscience."

"You're certainly no Wendell Wingate," she retorted, not backing down an inch.

He shook his head. "Ah, I hate to tell you this, but you're wrong."

"Oh?" she asked archly.

"Since we have yet to be formally introduced, you can't be expected to know my full name." He extended a hand to shake. "I'm Wendell Simon Wingate III."

"Are you serious?" She snorted a laugh, a sound he usually found distasteful. For some reason, when this woman did it, he wanted to crack a smile. Her hand flew up to cover her nose and mouth, and two spots of bright red appeared on her high cheekbones.

"I am always serious about meeting a pretty woman." He hit her with his best smile. "I'm new to town, and I appreciate you making me feel so welcome."

When she lowered her hand, a sheepish smile curved lush, full lips. Simon's gaze dropped to them, and he found he had a hard time tearing it away. "You are welcome here," she relented. "And I'm sorry. I'm—"

"Miffed?" he supplied.

She laughed again, and this time it rang clear and true. "Not the word I would have chosen."

"It was nothing personal, Deputy," he assured her in a low voice. "He retained me to be his counsel. You didn't have much of a case."

She opened her mouth to say something, but Darlene called for her. "Lori, honey? Your shakes are ready."

She stood her ground, her defiant glare locked on him. Simon found he didn't mind this particular woman's boldness. "You didn't have to take him on."

"You may not have noticed, but lawyers aren't thick on the ground here. At least, not defense attorneys."

She tipped her pointed chin up a notch. "He could have gone elsewhere for representation."

He leaned in and dropped his voice to a conspiratorial whisper. "Big-money clients are few and far between in these parts. I promised my granddad I wouldn't run the place into the ground in the first six months," he added with a wink. Simon winced inside. His mother would have tanned him for making such a tawdry move. "He's already handed all the Timber Masters business over to their new in-house counsel, so I've been tasked with keeping the place afloat."

Until a few months ago, the majority of the firm's business had come from the Masters family and their family-owned forestry and lumber business, Timber Masters. Marlee Masters had come home to roost after earning her law degree, and his grandfather got the notion to make a run at one of the elected posts on the circuit court. The timing of it all seemed… inevitable, if not exactly fortuitous.

The problem was, Simon wasn't sure he could keep his promise to his grandfather. Other than writing a new will for Eleanor Young, a timid divorcée who'd lost her only son earlier in the year, he hadn't done a single lawyerly thing since he'd moved to Pine Bluff. The call from Samuel Coulter needing someone local to represent his "various business and personal interests" had broken weeks of Dora reminding him his calendar was distressingly open.

"So, naturally, you scraped the bottom of the nearest barrel to find a client. Congratulations," she added as she shouldered past him to get to the pickup window. "You've got yourself a real winner there, Wingate."

Chapter Three

"Hi, Mama, I'm home," she called out as she walked through the back door of her childhood home.

Her mother shot her a bland look over her shoulder. "Hello, Lourdes."

Lori cringed at the formality of the greeting. Not long ago, she would have been *mija*. But everything had gone sideways when she moved out.

Sophia Castillo-Cabrera was not a woman who thawed quickly. Her mother added another unlabeled jar to the collection in the crook of her arm and straightened, letting the door swing shut without looking directly at Lori. "What brings you by?"

Lori quickly squashed the flash of hurt. Moving out of her girlhood home had started out as a bone of contention and had finally simmered down to a touchy subject. The family was still reeling from the death of her father and aunt in a car accident when they'd discovered Anita Cabrera had left her house to Lori in her will.

Her mother had expected Lori to sell the property and use the proceeds to help fund her younger siblings' education. Instead, she'd packed up her clothes and what few worldly possessions she'd accumulated since leaving the army and moved into the cozy bungalow.

Why couldn't her mother understand that Lori needed the freedom of living on her own for the first time in her life?

Her mother believed Lori was thumbing her nose at the family by moving out. Females were to stay in the family fold, living in the house of their father until they moved in with their spouse. Somehow, Sophia managed to skim over the years Lori had spent sleeping in military barracks. As far as she was concerned, her first-born child was besmirching the family name with her father and aunt barely gone a year.

Lori should have felt guilty, but she didn't. Which caused her even greater remorse.

Forcing a smile, she held up a plastic grocery bag. "I came by to drop off a couple of T-shirts for Lena." She made a face when her mother stared back at her, unreadable. "She said something about the military look being back in style."

"That's nice of you," her mother answered distractedly.

The gulf between them was widening, and Lori had no idea how to stop it. "Mama, I love you."

Her mother moved to the stove and stirred the sauce simmering there. "You love me so much you don't want to live under my roof."

"I was gone for four years and you never gave me a hard time," she pressed.

"Totally different."

"Not different. I am literally less than a mile away," she argued.

"I am aware," Sophia replied.

Lori sighed and repeated the same mantra she'd been using since the day Wendell Wingate almost apologetically informed them her aunt Anita had drawn up a will. "Mama, I'm a grown woman. I need space of my own."

Her mother's shoulders stiffened. "You don't think I was a grown woman when I married your father and moved into his house?"

This was a worn, old circular argument. She understood why her mother wanted her to sell the property. Sophia was worried about paying for school for the younger kids and expected Lori to dump the proceeds from the sale into the family coffers. But there was life insurance money, and Lori would help however she could. Sure, sometimes she felt selfish for hanging on to the place, but she couldn't help thinking Anita had known she needed her own space.

"I'll go find Lena," she said, gesturing to the narrow hallway.

She followed the thump-thump-snare roll of a pop song to the door decorated with a satin-and-ribbon memory board with *Marialena* spelled out in paste rhinestones and pearls. Casting her memory back, Lori tried to recall whether she'd ever had anything half as sparkly. She didn't think so. The most elaborate article of clothing she'd ever owned or worn was the sherbet-peach ball gown each of the Cabrera girls had worn for their quinceañera celebrations. Lori had complained to her mother about the flounces and lace. The previous year, Lena had moaned about not having a gown of her own. Lori had offered to pay for a new one, but neither her mother nor her sulking younger sister would hear of it, so she'd backed off.

A week after the party, her father and his sister had been driving home from a restaurant supply store in Albany when they were killed by a farmer from Prescott County who'd fallen asleep at the wheel and crossed the centerline.

The memory board jumped when she rapped twice, then called through the hollow-core door. "Hey, Lena-da-queena. I brought you some cool soldier-girl clothes."

The volume decreased and Lena called out a desultory "Come in."

Lori opened the door to find her sister stretched sideways across the twin beds Lena'd shoved together. She tried to stifle the pang of grief when she saw her sister had removed Lori's pictures and mementos from the walls and the frame of the old-fashioned vanity mirror. Although Lori had hardly given them a second thought in years, she couldn't help feeling stung when she saw the bare spots.

"Wow. You've rearranged."

Lena pressed the button on the side of her phone to lock the screen. She barely spared Lori a glance. "I figured you wouldn't care."

Lori couldn't help but be impressed by her sister's nonchalance. Everyone else in the family—her brothers included—had been insulted by her defection and been vocal in their opinions. But her sister held her cards close to her chest. Lena had always been quiet, far more reserved than the rest of them, which sometimes made Lori uncomfortable.

Her gaze traveled to the phone her sister had oh-so-casually locked and placed facedown on the bedspread, and Lori decided *reserved* wasn't exactly the right word for her baby sister. Lena was secretive. An island unto herself amid the noise and chaos of their family.

Without waiting for the invitation she was fairly sure wouldn't come, Lori strode into the room and dropped heavily onto the edge of the bed. "Did you have a bonfire or something?"

Lena shook her head, pointing to the closet. "Nah, I put it all in a box. It's there if you want it."

It hurt to have been erased from the room, but Lori was pleased her sister hadn't simply tossed her mementos in the trash. Pressing her hand to her throat, she massaged away the unexpected tightness she felt there. "Thanks. I'll take it with me," she said, striving to keep her voice light. "I brought you some shirts. One has the crossed-flintlock-pistols logo. Pretty cool," she said, dropping the grocery bag containing the army T-shirts onto the bed.

Lena frowned in puzzlement, and Lori wondered if she'd imagined their previous conversation. The one where her sister was waxing poetic about how cool it was that Lori'd been in the army, and how Lena could rock her new pair of khaki cargo pants if she just had the right shirt to go with them. The pucker between the younger girl's untweezed eyebrows deepened, and Lori felt the urge to rush to the kitchen and thank her mother for making her baby sister adhere to the same strict edicts she'd had to endure.

"You brought me some old shirts?" Lena said, enunciating with such a deep drawl the words almost sounded foreign and exotic.

Lori pursed her lips, willing herself not to snap. Lena might be quiet, but she was still capable of serving up heaping helpings of teenage snark. Only their father, who thought the sun rose and set on his precious baby girl, had been exempt from her contempt. If Sophia hadn't been giving her elder daughter such a hard time for wanting to live her life on her own terms, Lori was sorely tempted to actually jump up and run to the kitchen to give her mother a hug. Coming home to her family after years in the military helped her realize parenting was very much like engaging in hand-to-hand combat on a daily basis.

"You said you needed something to go with your cargo pants."

"So you brought me some hand-me-downs you probably sweated through, like, a hundred times?"

Tired from the bad start to the day and a shift filled with particularly annoying calls, Lori decided to disengage. She didn't want to snap at her sister and become more of an outlaw within her own family. Lori pushed off the bed, irked by the sneaking suspicion the teen was baiting her, and went to the closet to retrieve the shoebox of old photos, certificates and ribbons Lena had removed from the walls. "You know what…? Never mind."

With the box wedged under her arm, she was about to leave when she caught her sister peeking at her phone. Lena frowned at the screen, her bottom lip caught between her teeth. Suddenly, Lori saw a flash of the girl who used to crawl into her bed on Christmas Eves, worried Santa never got her letter.

"What's wrong, Le-Le?"

Her sister's face hardened for a millisecond, but she quickly crumbled. "It's Jasmine," she whispered.

The quaver in Lena's voice nearly broke Lori. She moved back to the bed and reclaimed her spot, setting the box at her feet. Reaching out, she placed a comforting hand on the younger girl's back. Lena and Jasmine had been inseparable since their preschool days. If her sister's bestie was in trouble, Lena would feel it too. "What's Jas up to these days?"

"She's, um…" Lena's gaze shifted to her phone as she weighed how much to divulge. "She's been, uh, blowing me off."

"No way."

"She is."

Crossing her legs at her ankles, Lori tried for disinterested nonchalance as she gently pressed. "Any idea why?"

Lena's lips tightened then trembled as she said, "She met some boy."

"I see. And she doesn't have time for you?" Lori asked, sympathetic. She recalled all too well how much it hurt when her own childhood friends started to drift away.

"She's all into this Rick guy. He's so smarmy. All muscly and tattooed." She wrinkled her nose in disapproval.

"Tattooed?"

Lori reared back. Pine Bluff may be the biggest town in Masters County, but it was hardly a booming metropolis. He must have lived outside of town. People around here tended to be conservative. Cleancut. At least on the surface.

Lori didn't have anything against tattoos. She herself had one of the crossed flintlock pistols of the military police emblem done the evening after their graduation. Her classmates had teased her for making the artist do hers about one-fifth the size of the sample. And on her hip. Sophia had walked into the bathroom as Lori was climbing from the shower one day and nearly fainted. Or so she claimed. She'd been an adult, but her mother had been horrified to discover her daughter had "ruined" her "beautiful" body.

But who would let their kid get all inked up at fifteen?

"Isn't he young to be getting tattoos?"

Lena shot her a scornful side-eye. "He's not our age."

"No?" Lori squawked.

"God, no. Boys our age are so…disgusting."

Lori couldn't argue with Lena's logic. Having grown up with younger brothers, Lori was all too aware of how unattractive fifteen-year-old boys could be. "I'm assuming he's older?"

Lena shrugged. "Eighteen or nineteen, maybe? Out of high school."

"Ah…wow," Lori murmured, her mind racing as she scrambled for a way to get back to the place where Lena felt comfortable confiding in her. "I guess I had no idea Jas was into older guys."

Lena stared hard at the phone but her face crumpled. "Me either. But she turned sixteen and she has her provisional license and can drive now, and I'm not good enough…" Her sister trailed off into a hiccuping sob.

"Oh, Le-Le." Twisting around, Lori pulled her sister into an awkward hug when the girl started to cry in earnest. She wanted to ask if Jasmine's parents knew she was flirting with some strange guy, but instinct told her she'd lose cool points for the question, and right now she wanted to keep Lena talking to her. "I'm sorry. I know it hurts."

Sixteen. Lori knew from experience it was a dangerous age. It marked the tipping point where parental approval started coming second to what your friends thought. When a girl's body started telling her she was a woman, and she was all too willing to believe the hype. Sixteen. It was the age of consent in Georgia, though Lori was fairly certain her sister and her friends couldn't even tell her what consent really meant. Her blood boiled and her heart raced as she squeezed Lena tighter, holding out hope that her sister would choose to remain on the "girl" side of that dividing line a little longer.

"I don't get why we can't be fr-friends anymore," Lena sobbed. "I'm cool," she added with a small hiccup.

"You are," Lori cooed, stroking the younger girl's silky hair. "You're the coolest."

Lena gave a watery laugh and tried to pull away, but Lori wouldn't let her go. Thankfully, Lena relaxed into the embrace, resting her cheek on her big sister's shoulder. "And the stupid thing is, she told him she's seventeen. Like that makes a big difference. She doesn't even look seventeen."

Lori swallowed the lump in her throat. "No, she doesn't."

And it made no difference in the eyes of the law. But in the life of a young woman, those tender years mattered. Lori remembered them all too well. The confusion. The heady power that came from being noticed by boys for the first time. The constant roller-coaster ride of emotion. The tug-of-war between what her friends were doing and what her parents expected of her. Oh, the drama. And most of all, the aching desire to get adolescence over with so she could get on with what she once thought of as "real life."

"She's too young to be fooling around with guys of any age."

"It's gross," Lena retorted.

Lori couldn't help but smile a little as she smoothed her sister's hair. "That too."

"And I don't think they're even really going out. I mean, they text and she sends him messages on PicturSpam and stuff, but she's—" Lena drew a shuddering breath "—she's blowing me off, and I miss her.

We've been friends forever, and now she doesn't have time to text me back."

"I get it," Lori assured her. "Stinks."

"And he's so…gross."

Lori chuckled softly at her sister's choice of adjective. "It sucks when you see your friend hanging out with a guy who's…gross."

Her baby sister's giggle was a balm. "It's the perfect word," Lena insisted. "Get this. He has this job where he takes snakes around to these weird churches and stuff. Can you think of a nastier job? Jasmine went to a tent revival with her mee-maw and now she's all into him." Lena shuddered and Lori froze. "I guess they must pay okay and all, but ew. He works for the millionaire guy who owns the snake place they advertise on the highway. The Reptile Rendezvous?"

Lori held her sister tighter. "Oh, yeah?" she replied, her voice weak.

She wrinkled her nose. "Yeah. All the kids are talking about that place. That's why they're all dressing in camo and safari stuff. Like they think it's so cool."

"They do?"

"Yeah. I think it's mostly because the guy is so rich and all," she said with a shrug. "I really don't get it, but Jasmine's all worked up about him."

This time, Lori pulled back, needing to read her sister's face. "The snake guy? Coulter?"

Lena scowled. "No. Yeah. I mean, his name is Rick. Weren't you listening?"

"Right, yeah, Rick. The tatted-up snake guy," Lori

confirmed, relief washing through her at the realization her sister's friend was at least one step removed from Coulter's clutches.

"If you do get Jas to text you back, tell her Lori said to ditch the snake guy—he's too old for her. And to stay away from Reptile Rendezvous."

Lena snorted. "Yeah, right. I'm her best friend. If she won't listen to me, she's sure not gonna listen to you."

"Yeah, well, I'm her BFF's big sister, which makes me kind of hers too." She gave Lena another squeeze, then grabbed the shoebox as she rose. "Just keep trying with her, Le-Le. That's all you can do."

"I will."

Lori backed out of the room with a smile and a wave, determined to give Jasmine's parents a heads-up. Jas was playing a dangerous game, and even if she was considered old enough in the eyes of the law, she wasn't in reality. Someone needed to try to help Jasmine make better, smarter choices.

If Lori couldn't help with that, she could always go in another direction. She would bet this Rick guy didn't know or care about the legalities. She might be able to scare him off, if Jasmine's parents didn't beat her to it.

Passing through the kitchen, she asked, "Mama? Do you have Keely Jones's phone number? I think Jasmine might want some of my shirts too," she fibbed.

"In my phone," Sophia replied, waving a spoon toward the kitchen table without looking up.

Lori used her parents' wedding anniversary date

to unlock her mother's phone and quickly forwarded Jasmine's mother's contact information to her own phone. The moment she set the mobile back on the table, her mother appeared at her side with a plastic container.

"Here. You can have these for supper."

Lori smiled, kissed her mother on the cheek and graciously accepted the warm-from-the-oven enchiladas. "Thank you." As she headed out the back door, she called back another "I love you, Mama" just for good measure, then headed for her car.

She left the house wondering if her stomach would ever stop roiling enough for her to eat a bite of those delicious-smelling enchiladas. Climbing into her car, she placed the box of mementos and food container on the passenger seat. Gripping the steering wheel tight, she counted to four as she drew a breath in, held it for four, then let it go slowly.

She drove to the end of the block, hooked a right, then pulled to the curb. Out of sight of her childhood home, Lori took her phone from her pocket and pulled up the contact information. As she waited for Jasmine's mother to answer, she gnawed her lip. Her intervention in the teenager's life would most definitely be unwelcome, but she had a duty. When the other woman answered, cheerful in her oblivion, Lori knew in her gut she was doing the right thing. The last thing she wanted was to find her sister's best friend walking down the side of Highway 19, scared and crying. Or worse.

Chapter Four

The following morning, Simon was heading for the district attorney's office when he ran into Deputy Cabrera in the atrium. Well, he didn't run into her so much as she stopped dead in front of him and directed her death-ray stare at him. "Good morning," he said politely.

The deputy narrowed her eyes warily and he fought back the urge to smirk. Her expression said any smiling or smirking would be completely unwelcome. And, well, for some reason, he wanted her to welcome seeing him.

"Good morning."

They stood staring at one another awkwardly. At last, Simon gestured to the door behind him. "I was heading to a meeting with District Attorney Hayes."

"Good for you."

He ignored her smart remark and switched to a different tactic. "When I was talking to him the other day, he told me about the methamphetamine problems you all have been sorting out these past few years."

She pursed her lips. "I'm surprised you didn't hear

about those cases from your grandfather. Wendell handled the defense for most of the accused. At least, those who were locals. Maybe he figured you wouldn't be interested in Pine Bluff news."

Simon swallowed a wince. People around here had a way of making it clear they disapproved of his absence from his grandparents' lives without coming out and saying so.

"I suppose it was sort of abstract for me," he answered honestly.

She crossed her arms over her chest and widened her stance. The combative move should have made her more intimidating, but perversely enough, Simon found it attractive. He had always been attracted to women who weren't afraid to stand their ground.

His mother might look the ultimate politician's wife on the outside, but there was no question who ruled the roost. Simon had been raised to respect women. In a weird way, Deputy Cabrera reminded him of his mother, though the two of them couldn't have been more opposite in appearance and demeanor. Bettina Wingate was petite, blonde and perfectly put together.

Lourdes Cabrera was also petite, but the similarities ended there. She was curvy. Shapely. She reminded him of those World War Two–era pinups guys painted on the fuselage of their planes. He'd only seen her in uniform, but her figure was impossible to hide.

And she made those curves look dangerous. Powerful. This woman couldn't play the delicate Southern flower if she tried. She was commanding, with her intense dark stare and the utility belt stuffed with weaponry. Don't think he hadn't noted how the nylon belt hugged her rounded hips.

Hooking a thumb over his shoulder, he said, "Well, either way, I got my first taste of how seriously people feel about drug trafficking in these parts early this morning."

She nodded, her expression sober. "The Showalters called you, I'll bet. I heard Mike busted Timmy Showalter for possession with the intent to distribute last night."

The corner of Simon's mouth kicked up. Though he'd spoken with his client for only five minutes, there was absolutely no doubt in Simon's mind that the story the kid was feeding him was complete BS. Good thing it wasn't Simon's job to believe him or not. It was Simon's job to make sure he had an adequate defense. "My client has absolutely no idea how those pills ended up in his backpack. This was his first offense, and he's a minor."

Her frown deepened. "He's seventeen. Timmy and my brother Lorenzo are in the same class. They were in Cub Scouts together."

Simon wanted to kick himself for sounding so cavalier about the kid's arrest and the seriousness of the charges. It was easy to be flippant when one didn't have a relationship with the people one was representing. He had to remember he wasn't in Atlanta anymore. With the metropolis's booming population, it seemed hardly anyone was a local. Almost everyone he came across in this town was someone to somebody else.

He felt a brief longing for his old boring job of cajoling senators and representatives on behalf of special-interest groups. In politics, the lives hanging in the balance were far more removed than those in his present situation. In politics, you had to watch your every step. Even if you were playing within bounds, there was always someone who would spin the angle to suit them. He'd learned that the hard way.

"I'm sorry. It must be tough seeing a kid you watched grow up get into trouble. I'll do my best for him."

"Please do."

Simon took a deep, steadying breath. In any other jurisdiction, a cop would be hoping Simon's client got the book thrown at him. Hard. Here, she wanted him to do a good job defending the kid. The fact of the matter was, he wasn't entirely sure he was going to be any good at providing adequate defense to people he felt were absolutely guilty.

He'd lain awake for hours the previous night thinking about Coulter's cold eyes, and the smug, reflexive smile the man wore like a mask. Perhaps it was simply because Coulter had money and was used to getting his way, or perhaps he was born a supercilious ass. Either way, the man's attitude didn't settle well with Simon.

She unfurled her arms and let them fall to rest on her belt. "To be honest, I don't get how you defense attorneys do it," she said, shaking her head in slow wonder. "I spent a lot of time trying to lure your grandfather away from the dark side."

Surprised, Simon gazed at the woman. "We have all the cookies," he replied, falling back on flirtation.

Wendell had never mentioned anything about the sheriff's officers other than to commend the work Ben Kinsella and his crew did in picking up the pieces after the Drug Enforcement Administration left the county in tatters.

"You and Wendell were friends?" he asked, hating the suspicious roil of his stomach.

Her narrow gaze became distinctly disdainful. "Yes, Wendell and I are friends," she replied, correcting his tense. She spun on her heel and headed for the sheriff's office. She'd about reached the door when she paused and looked back at him.

Simon froze, arrested by the intensity in her eyes. "Was there something else, Deputy?"

"Yes." She let her hand fall away from the door handle and took two steps back in his direction. Simon silently willed her to take more, but she stopped. The rubber soles of her utility boots squeaked on the tile floor when she drew to a halt. "How well acquainted are you with the people who work for your client?"

Simon was not at all surprised by the derisive tone she used when she spoke the word *client*. He got her meaning, but he needed her to be more direct.

"I'm not sure I'm following the question," he replied cautiously.

"The people who work for Coulter. Have you, uh,

met any of them?" she asked, hitting him with her impenetrable dark gaze.

He shook his head. "I have not. I am not well enough acquainted with people around here to identify who works where and for whom. Why do you ask?"

Deputy Cabrera hesitated. For the first time since he'd laid eyes on her, he saw her fidget.

Granted, it was a small tell. Her fingers toyed with the Velcro closure on one of the compartments on her belt. A nervous twitch of her hand he might not have noticed if it weren't for the ripping of Velcro hooks tearing through the silence between them. Over and over again, she opened the flap, then smoothed it down again. He hoped it wasn't the pocket with a Taser or similar weapon.

"I'm worried about my younger sister," she began abruptly, jolting him from his study of her nervous movements.

"You are?"

She wagged her head, stunned to find herself confiding in him.

"Well, not her… One of her friends."

Sensing she was struggling, he fell back on doing what lawyers do best—ask questions until the person unwittingly tells everything.

"How many siblings do you have?" he asked, keeping his question light and friendly.

"Five. Four brothers and one sister."

The rigidity in her stance and the succinct answer told him she hadn't wanted to disclose any more information. His breath caught when he saw the pretty pink wash of a blush flare high on her cheeks. Obliged by his upbringing, he did the gentlemanly thing and helped her out of the corner she'd talked herself into. "Your sister is how old?"

"Fifteen. She's a sophomore. Her name is Lena."

"Pretty name." He made a motion for her to go on.

"Lena has a friend. They've been friends since they were in preschool. Her name is Jasmine."

She stopped there, and Simon waited patiently. He got the feeling Deputy Cabrera wasn't accustomed to confiding secrets. He was certain it was costing her more than she let on to share information with him, of all people. He was fairly sure she'd pegged him as public enemy number one.

"Jasmine. Got it."

She wanted something from him. Needed his assistance in some way. And when a woman as competent as Deputy Cabrera asked for help, a smart man sat up and took notice, because something big had to be weighing on her.

"Her friend is…kind of hanging around a guy who works for your client."

The way she spit the words *your client* at him made him flinch.

"I see." He scowled. "She's fifteen, you say?"

"Jasmine is sixteen, but this guy… From what Lena tells me, he's older."

"And you want me to poke around and see if any of the guys who work for Coulter have been in trouble?"

No sooner had the words left his mouth than she

threw up her hands and backed off again. "You know what? Never mind."

He took a step closer, and when she didn't back away, he pressed. "I'm not your enemy. You asked for help. I'm willing to help."

"You know what? I don't need your help," she snapped.

"Deputy, I'm doing the exact same job Wendell would have done. I'm not the bad guy here."

"I don't think you are," she answered a shade too quickly.

This time he couldn't repress his smile. "You do, but I'm going to do my best to convince you you've got me all wrong."

"Why do you care?" she asked, bristling.

"Because I want us to be friends," he answered.

"Why?" she asked again. This time, the single word sounded bewildered. Simon saw his opening and was careful to tread lightly.

"I don't have any friends here," he said, opting for the blunt approach. "Being new in town and all, I would prefer to have more friends than enemies." He made sure he was looking straight into her eyes. "And we are on the same side, Lourdes."

"Lori."

Simon fought the urge to grin because her expression was so expressively solemn. She'd offered him the diminutive, and damn it, he was going to take it. "Lori," he corrected.

She blinked, breaking the connection between them. "I don't understand how you figure we're on the same side. Hayes and I, we're on the same side. But you…" She shook her head. "I can't understand how defense attorneys can defend people they know are up to no good."

"We can do it because everybody has a right to an advocate," he said, repeating the party line his law professors hammered home about the topic. "It's all about checks and balances. It doesn't mean I'm on their side or condoning heinous and criminal behavior."

She chuckled and gave her head a shake. "You contradict yourself, Counselor."

"Simon," he interjected.

"Simon," she amended with a jut of her pointed chin.

He wanted to ask her to say his name again, but based on the conversation they were having, he didn't think she'd be inclined to indulge him. So, he fell back on another of his grandfather's favorite sayings.

"There are some who say the defense attorney is the only person without an agenda in the courtroom."

"Yeah, Wendell used to use the same con. He didn't have any better luck getting me to swallow the line than you will."

She backed off a step and reached for the door again. Rather than fleeing into the offices of the sheriff's department, she glanced back again. Simon mentally snapped a picture of her. With her expressive dark eyes and the heavy knot of hair pinned tightly to her nape, she was utterly arresting.

"I understand what you're saying, and I'm aware this isn't an easy town to live in when you're an outsider."

The phrasing of her statement was almost as compelling as the husky rasp in her voice. He cocked his head and waited for more. Prayed there'd be more.

She gave the door handle a yank. "We won't be enemies, but I'm not so sure about the friends thing."

He nodded and shoved his hands into the pockets of his suit pants, not caring if he ruined the line of the tailoring. "I'll take not-enemies for now."

She ducked into the office, and the door swished shut behind her on its hydraulic hinge. He withdrew his hands from his pockets and looked around at the municipal building's dormant atrium, wondering if the budget was so tight they couldn't afford to at least run the fountain.

They weren't going to be enemies, he repeated to himself as he studied the pattern in the mosaic tiles. He would work on the friends part. He would, because something told him Lori would be a good friend to have. She had already shown herself to be fierce and protective. She was asking after some guy who was messing with a friend of her sister. She was obviously the type to be loyal and unwavering in her companionship. It sure couldn't hurt to have a friend in this insular town.

Christ. He scrubbed a hand over his face. He didn't want her to see how conflicted he truly was. Simon didn't want to go poking around in his client's personnel records. He hadn't expected to find all this...

unsavory stuff here in Pine Bluff. Had his grandfather spent his entire life defending drug dealers and perverts? How did the old man sleep at night?

The outer door opened and Simon physically shook himself out of that line of thinking as the district attorney walked in. Simon gave Harrison Hayes a closer inspection this time. He'd been too blinded by Coulter and the potentially hefty billable hours to pay much attention to the man he'd be facing in court on a fairly regular basis. To his relief, Hayes looked much like the guys Simon had come through undergrad and law school with. In other words, he wore a decent suit, kept his shoes polished, leaned conservative in the barber's chair, and his sharply intelligent eyes caught everything.

The prosecutor drew up short when he saw Simon standing there. "Did we have a meeting?"

Simon gave the other man a wan smile. "I'm here to represent Timothy Showalter," he announced.

Hayes headed toward the door opposite the sheriff's department, what Simon had earmarked the justice side of the county's law and justice headquarters. The second floor of the municipal building held the county clerk, emergency management, economic development and finance offices. Fire and rescue were housed in a prefabricated building on the edge of town.

Holding back, he watched as the DA pulled a key ring from his pocket and juggled his briefcase from one hand to the other. "Come in. We'll talk."

What Lori had said about the guy messing with the high school girl niggled at Simon. "Have you guys had a lot of trouble coming out of Coulter's place?" he asked when the other man swung the door open wide.

"I wouldn't say a lot," Hayes equivocated. With a practiced swipe of his hand, he switched on the fluorescent lights. "There was the girl Lori picked up the other night. A few of the local teenagers have scored weekend jobs out there, so that's made it something of a hot spot. Some have tried to sneak in."

Simon blinked, giving his pupils time to adjust to the sudden brightness after standing in the dim atrium. Glancing back, he realized not only was the fountain drained dry, but also the two-story lobby itself was lit only by skylights and the glow spilling from the glass-walled offices surrounding it. "The refuge is open to the public."

"Only on weekends and for the price of admission," Hayes answered. "Some people don't care to pay admission. Mostly it's been kids daring each other to sneak in and that sort of thing. Up until recently, Coulter's been cool with letting Ben put the fear of the law into them, but now that he's retained you, who knows. We may be seeing more trespassing charges pop up." He motioned for Simon to follow. "Come on back."

With a jerk, Simon dragged himself from the doorway and followed the other man into his office. He wanted to press harder, find out exactly what Masters County's law and justice departments had run into with Coulter before he'd been retained, but frankly, he was more than ready to deal with a case that didn't involve his biggest client.

Hayes pulled a file from his briefcase and flipped it open.

"Timothy Showalter. Seventeen years old, first offense. Charged with possession with intent to distribute," Hayes recited without looking down at the page once. "Deputy Schaeffer says he was holding the bag in his hand and showing it to some friends when he approached. When he spotted Mike coming, Timmy shoved it back into his backpack. He tried to tell the deputy he'd need a search warrant to look in there."

The two men shared a chuckle. Simon made a mental note to tell Timothy Showalter not to take TV legal dramas too seriously. He needed a civics lesson on the basics of search and seizure.

"He says he has no idea how it got into his backpack, and he was showing it to his friends to ask if they put it there."

"Mmm-hmm," the DA hummed. At last, he dropped his gaze to the file and skimmed the police report. "If your client agrees, I'm willing to go with a plea of nolo contendere under the First Time Offender Act."

"We'd ask the judge for a conditional discharge of probation plus community service in lieu of jail time," Simon countered.

Hayes nodded and closed the file. "I can agree to those terms." Sighing, he dropped heavily into his chair. "I hate sending kids to jail for being stupid." He looked up at Simon, his expression hard. "You tell him this is his one get-out-of-jail-free card. People around these parts are pretty edgy when it comes to any kind of drug dealing. They may look the other way if I let one of their own slide on some weed, but if he's busted again, I will come after him before the townsfolk can come after me with pitchforks. We clear?"

"Crystal."

Hayes nodded, then reached up to shake Simon's hand. "I hate starting the day this way. Timmy Showalter lives down the street from me. His mama called my house at least three times last night begging me not to send her baby to prison. Apparently, Timmy sleeps with a scrap of his old security blanket."

Simon nodded, keeping his expression carefully neutral. "I will make sure he is aware that if there is a next time, he will feel the full weight of the law *and* his mama. I'll also threaten to leak the information about his blankie."

The two men exchanged wary smiles.

"I'll talk to my client, speak to his parents and get back to you by the end of the day," Simon promised.

"I'm surprised Barb Showalter isn't blowing up your phone already. She says he's been giving her nothing but trouble ever since he went to work at the Reptile Rendezvous, and everyone knows you're Coulter's guy."

"I am not 'Coulter's guy,' and I keep my phone on silent mode," Simon said gruffly.

"Probably wise."

Unease crept up Simon's spine as he made a mental note to ask Mrs. Showalter exactly what kind of trouble young Timmy had become since taking the job at the refuge. "I'll, uh, I'll speak with her about her concerns when I call to talk about the plea."

"Good."

There was a note of finality in Hayes's response, and it jerked Simon from his thoughts. He eyed the DA warily, but found he was in no hurry to leave. Frankly, he was tired of talking to himself…and Dora. He wanted to make some friends in this town, and what better place to start than with the man across the desk. After all, there was nothing wrong with being friendly adversaries. If he won the district attorney over to his side, maybe he could get beautiful Lori Cabrera to stop giving him the stink eye each time their paths crossed.

Rubbing his cheek, he ventured out onto the limb. "I was thinking of inviting some people over to watch the game Saturday. I'll fire up Wendell's old Weber grill and all." He made a vague, all-encompassing gesture. "I'd like you to come, if you're free." Hayes looked up, his surprise evident. Simon tossed off a nonchalant shrug. "I was going to invite Sheriff Kinsella and Marlee Masters, whoever's not on duty across the hall…"

He prayed Mike Schaeffer would be on shift at kick-off time. Not because he had anything against the guy, but he was more anxious to see Lori again. It occurred to him she might not be available. He hadn't spotted a wedding ring. A lack of jewelry didn't mean anything. For all he knew, she could be involved with Hayes.

"Hey, I didn't even ask," he blurted. "Are you married? Seeing someone? Either way, you're welcome to bring a plus-one or something."

Hayes looked taken aback by the question. "Yeah, uh, no. I'm not married. Sure, I'll come over to watch the game. Need me to bring anything?"

Simon's mind raced and he started to panic at the thought of throwing an impromptu party together. Then he remembered Dora. For the first time since he'd arrived in Pine Bluff, he blessed his grandfather's longtime secretary's almost compulsive need to assist him. She could help him pull this together. And Miss Delia, Wendell's mostly retired housekeeper.

"Uh, no. I don't think so. I was going to keep it simple—burgers, dogs and stuff."

Hayes nodded. "Cool. I'll bring some soft drinks and beer. Maybe some chips."

"That would be great." Simon began to back out of the room. "I need to double-check the schedule. I think we have a six-o'clock kickoff."

"It is."

Simon stifled the urge to chuckle. This was Southeastern Conference football country. He wouldn't be surprised if everyone in town had the Georgia Bulldogs football schedule memorized whether they were fans or not.

"I'll have the charcoal ready."

"Sounds good."

"Great." Simon nodded enthusiastically. "See you Saturday."

"Yep." Hayes smirked and fired up his laptop. "The sooner you talk to your client about the deal, the better. I don't keep my phone on Silent, and I get annoyed when helicopter parents try to land on my head."

"Gotcha." Simon beat a path out of the man's office. He had a party to plan.

Chapter Five

Deputy Steve Wasson of Prescott County called to give her a heads-up. An Amber Alert was being issued. Fourteen-year-old Kaylin Bowers had been reported missing by her parents when they woke up to find their daughter's rumpled bed empty. Lori stared at the computer screen, studying the photos the girl's parents had collected. Most were the usual posed shots taken at school, but the one Steve sent through was different from the others. This was a selfie pulled from a PicturSpam account Kaylin's parents had no clue she'd opened.

One in which fourteen-year-old Kaylin claimed to be an eighteen-year-old model and actress. In the photo unearthed by the techy deputy at the Prescott County Sheriff's Department, she looked every day of eighteen.

"Like waving a red cloth to a predator," Lori murmured to herself. "Was I that trusting at that age?"

Lori didn't ponder the question long. Her parents had been strict with her—something she remembered chafing against, but was now thankful for in retrospect. Teenagers in general were given to poor impulse control, something she'd had to bite her tongue to keep from pointing out when Steve told her Kaylin's parents didn't monitor her social media accounts closely because they didn't want to "invade" their daughter's privacy. Lori would bet her badge they were regretting not being nosier now.

She was pulling up her own PicturSpam account to do some stalking when the door to the sheriff's office opened and Simon Wingate walked in. Minimizing the window, Lori watched in amazement as Julianne, their normally unflappable dispatcher, flittered and fluttered, practically cooing her hellos to the man. Their determined flirtation was so painful to watch, Lori felt the need to put one or both—or all of them—out of their misery.

"Don't you have any work to do?" she demanded, glaring at Wingate. "I can call fire and rescue. Maybe they'll let you chase an ambulance around for a while so you can stay in business."

Her snark cut through Julianne's excitement like a hot knife.

Simon didn't fluster easily. He simply smiled and said, "Great idea! I've been looking for a good gym around here. I guess y'all make your own CrossFit, huh?"

Lori was still coming up with a retort when he raised a hand in greeting to Ben, who was lounging in his chair, watching them go at each other. "Hey, Sheriff, how's it going?"

"It's going well as can be expected," Ben answered laconically. "What brings you in, Counselor?"

Simon smiled so wide a boyish dimple appeared in his left cheek. "Call me Simon."

Lori wanted to sneer at him and his stupid dimple, but she couldn't. She wanted to touch it, which might explain why the mere sight of the flirty dent made her agitated.

"I come in peace." He raised both hands high in surrender. "I was across the hall talking to the DA, and I realized I hadn't socialized with anyone since I moved here."

Lori scoffed. "I'm sure you think we were all feeling the loss keenly."

He aimed the full wattage of his charming smile on her, and she almost fell back in her seat. "Well, the thought had crossed my mind, so I thought I'd put you all out of your misery and let you get to know me."

Julianne laughed out loud. "You're every bit the rascal you were when you were twelve years old," she cooed. "You remember the time your grandmama paid me to keep an eye on you for a couple of hours so she and your granddad could go to the spaghetti supper at the church? Your granddad was a deacon, and you were the devil incarnate."

"Remember?" Simon dropped a wink at the dispatcher. "I had the biggest crush on you, Miss Julianne."

"Liar," she purred.

"No." Simon shook his head vehemently. "No lie. I was twelve and you were seventeen, and I thought you were the prettiest thing I'd ever seen in my whole life."

Julianne went back to her keyboard, a primly pleased smile twitching the corners of her mouth. "I'll let you go on thinking I was only seventeen to your twelve."

Simon guffawed. "There is no way on earth I'm going to believe there's a bigger gap between us."

Lori almost growled. Julianne was at least ten years older than Simon Wingate. She was twelve years older than Lori herself, and Lori was fully capable of doing the math.

"Anyway," Simon said, interrupting her thoughts, "I came by to invite you all over to watch the football game on Saturday night. Granddad left his grill on the patio, and I'm capable of scorching some hamburgers." He added a winsome smile to the assault. "If y'all would come by, I'd be much obliged. It gets pretty quiet in the old house on the weekends."

Lori felt a pang of pity for the man, and it irked her. Pity was exactly what he'd been counting on. He was new in town, and he probably was lonely. She wasn't a fan of being cajoled into anything, and this whole barbecue setup reeked of manipulation.

"I'll speak to Marlee and see if she has any plans for Saturday night," Ben answered.

"Do that," Simon implored. "I ran into her at the Piggly Wiggly the other day. She was in a rush, so we didn't do much more than exchange hellos. I'm sure she has her hands full with Timber Masters now that her daddy is semiretired."

Semiretired. Lori noted the terminology. Henry Masters, Marlee's father and the man who practically ran the whole town, had had a debilitating stroke in the spring. Marlee had stepped in to take over the reins at the lumber company that kept many residents of the county employed.

"She does, but I'm making sure she takes time off. A cookout sounds great," Ben said agreeably.

"Great!" Simon's expression sobered, and the shine in his blue eyes seemed to dim a shade. "Marlee, Jeff and I used to run around together when we were kids, see what trouble we could find. Hard to believe Jeff is gone."

Lori ducked her head. In the past year, Pine Bluff had lost some of their best and brightest to a wannabe drug kingpin's power play. One of those men had been Marlee's brother, Jeff. The man Lori had been falling for. The one who had died in a tragic tangle of unsavory circumstances. She could feel Ben staring at the back of her neck and held herself still. She refused to let her discomfiture show.

Oblivious to the undercurrents, Simon blathered on. "I look forward to getting reacquainted with Marlee. And yourself, of course."

Lori wanted to chuckle at the man's attempt at a save, but the mere mention of Jeff Masters dampened her ability to laugh. Instead, she drew a deep breath when she lifted her head again. Big mistake. Simon Wingate was staring at her.

"I realize some people see us as being on opposite sides..." Only a fool would miss the tiny smirk that twitched his lips. "I don't believe we are. Sure, we have different functions within the judicial system, but at the end of the day, we're all after justice."

Lori opened her mouth to make a scathing comment, but Ben cut her off.

"You're absolutely right. I've been on the other side of the table, and all too aware of exactly how important it is to have someone sitting by your side when people are coming after you."

Lips thinning into a line, Lori studied her boss. Ben's expression remained open and inviting. She couldn't help but marvel at his perspective. Ben had once been an undercover agent for the Drug Enforcement Administration, but his cover had been blown in a bust gone horribly wrong. He'd been doubted, questioned and practically tossed away by the agency he'd given years of his life to serving. If such a thing were to happen to her, Lori doubted she'd be philosophical about it.

"I'll speak to Marlee, and give Dora a call to let you know if we can make it," Ben said evenly. "Can we bring anything?"

Simon inclined his head. "Cool. Uh—" he pointed toward the office across the lobby "—Hayes is bringing drinks. I'm not sure…" He trailed off with a shrug. "Whatever else you think we might want."

"We'll swing by the bakery and bring some dessert. Marlee's always up for something sweet," Ben offered.

"Awesome. Great." Simon clapped once and pivoted toward Julianne. "You in?"

She shook her head sadly. "I'm afraid we can't. My mother-in-law is doing poorly and we're going up to Macon to check in and spell Dylan's sister off for a couple of days."

"I'm sorry. You'll be missed," Simon replied, and oddly enough, he sounded sincere.

Lori clenched her teeth and closed her eyes, physically willing herself to stop thinking the worst of this man. He was right; he wasn't doing anything wrong. If his clients were the scum of the earth, that didn't mean he was. Did it?

She opened her eyes to find Simon staring at her. "Deputy Lori?"

The way he drawled her name both excited and annoyed her. She opened her mouth to say something smart, but all she said was "Saturday is my day off."

To her horror, she realized that rather than coming across as an excuse, it sounded like she had unlimited availability. She hastened to correct the impression.

"I plan to spend the day with my younger sister." It wasn't exactly a lie. The thought had crossed her mind that she needed to spend some quality time with Lena, and when she saw the photographs of Kaylin Bowers, she'd vowed to make it happen.

"The game doesn't start till six, and you're welcome to bring anyone along. I assure you we will keep things family friendly. My first soirée back in Pine Bluff can't be some kind of Roman orgy."

Lori's cheeks heated with a fiery flush. Julianne hooted and Ben let out a snort of laughter. A part of her couldn't believe he'd actually uttered the word *orgy* out loud. The devil on her shoulder told her it was completely on brand for Simon and the people he chose to defend.

"I'll keep the invitation in mind," she replied, enunciating each word carefully. Then she tacked a belated "Thank you" on, but it tasted grudging on her tongue.

Ben shot her a look, but she couldn't be bothered wasting the niceties on Simon Wingate. Not when the man made her feel so knotted up inside.

"Great, well, I'll see whoever can make it." He backed away. "Oh, and I assume Deputy Schaeffer will be on duty, but would you make sure to tell him to swing by to check on the score? We'll load him up with something to eat."

"Will do," Ben answered with a nod.

Simon lifted his hand in farewell. "Y'all have a nice day."

The door shut behind him and Julianne whirled on her. "Girl, are you blind? What the devil is wrong with you?"

Bristling, Lori glared back at her. "I'm not blind, and there's nothing wrong with me."

"There must be, because a gorgeous man walked in here specifically to ask you to come over to his house for a get-together and you… Ugh! What am I going to do with you?" Julianne cried.

"You do not have to do anything with me, and he did not come in here specifically for me. He invited everyone," Lori shot back. Behind her, Ben chuckled. Swiveling in her seat, she glared at her boss. "What?"

"I'm gonna have to side with Julianne on this one. I'm pretty sure she and I were not his target audience."

Lori splayed her hands. "He said he invited Hayes."

"Okay, so maybe it's a toss-up between you and Harry," Julianne said tartly. "Get in there and fight, girl. You think handsome single guys plop themselves down in friggin' Pine Bluff, Georgia, every day?"

"It's not a toss-up," Ben said. "Harry is an excuse, and Marlee and I are cover. Though, now that I think about it, he may have been counting on you for a covered dish or something, Julianne." Ben zoomed in on Lori. "How are your baked beans?" he teased.

The question earned him a wadded-up piece of paper tossed directly at his head. "They're delicious, but I may not want to share them."

Ben was not deterred. "The point is, he specifically asked you."

"He said I could bring anybody I wanted. I could bring a date."

Ben shook his head. "Oh, no. Not cool. Go or don't go, but don't bring a date," he advised.

Lori gaped, looking from Julianne to Ben and back again. "I don't get it. What are you two picking up on that I'm not? What makes you think he's concerned about whether I come or not?"

"I can't speak for Ben and his masculine intuition…" Julianne paused and her smile softened. "But I'd say it's because he looks at you the same way he used to look at me when he was seven—I mean, twelve."

Lori was surprised by how receptive Lena was to spending the day with her on Saturday, but when the teenager slid into her car, Lori suspected there'd been an ulterior motive behind Lena's eagerness. Eyeballing her sister as she settled into the passenger seat, she asked, "What has you all perky?"

Lena shook her head a tad too vigorously. "Nothing. I'm excited to spend the day with you."

The bright, cheerful greeting was so out of character with everything Lori had heard come out of her sister's mouth for the past six months, it set her antennae vibrating. "Uh-huh."

She put the car in gear and checked over her shoulder as she pulled away from the curb and her mother's house. "Okay. Hey, do you want me to take you somewhere to practice driving? Or maybe up and down some back roads? You have your permit on you, don't you?"

"Yes, but the permit says I can only drive with a parent or guardian."

Lori cut her sister a sidelong glance. "You might have heard—I have an in with the cops in this town," she said dryly.

Lena gasped in mock horror. "You're suggesting we break the law?"

"Never mind. It was only an idea." She drummed her fingers on the steering wheel. "So, what do you want to do today?"

Her sister clapped her hands together and whispered in an excited rush, "I think we should go to the Reptile Rendezvous."

Lori reared back, wrinkling her nose at the thought of going anywhere near Samuel Coulter's place. "What? Why?"

"Because I want to get a look at it," Lena insisted. "It's all anyone at school is talking about, plus the whole deal with Jasmine."

"Right," Lori said slowly, hating herself for warming to the idea.

"I want to go and see what the big whoop is," Lena said, a note of wheedling undercutting her overenthusiastic response.

"Honey, going there is not a great idea."

"You asked what I wanted to do today. This is what I want to do." In a blink, the chipper girl who'd greeted her was gone.

She slowed the car to a roll, but Lena seemed oblivious. She jolted them to a stop at the corner, garnering her sister's full, if sullen, attention. "You want to do this?" she asked, pinning Lena with a pointed stare. "It could be supercreepy there."

Her younger sister rolled her eyes. "Of course it's going to be creepy—it's full of snakes."

In a half-hearted attempt to steer their day toward something brighter, Lori offered a tempting alternative. "I could drive you up to the mall," she said enticingly.

Lena chewed her lip, clearly weighing the pros and cons of wheedling a new top or two out of Lori's last paycheck versus getting an eyeful of the guy her best friend was ditching her for.

Finally, Lena heaved a sigh and said, "They're only open to the public on Saturdays and Sundays. It might sound stupid, but I need to see this guy." When Lori started to answer, Lena held up a hand. "I know, I've seen his pictures online, but I want to see him live and in person. I have to see if he's all that." Her dark eyes were bright with unshed tears. "Why is he so special he's worth ditching twelve years of friendship?"

"Oh, honey." Lori reached across and gave her sister's hand a squeeze. "I wish I had the right things to say."

Her sister gave a watery laugh. "There's nothing to say. And I need to see why everyone is making such a big deal about this place. Half the kids at school are trying to get jobs there. It's all anyone talks about. It has to be because it's so creepy, right? With the snakes?"

Lori could hear the tears clogging Lena's throat, so she swallowed her own apprehension and hooked a left, heading for the highway. "You're probably right. If you think it will make you feel better, we'll go get creeped out together."

Twenty minutes later, she approached the sign directing them to the parking area for the Reptile Rendezvous, wondering for the hundredth time whose palm Coulter had greased to get the permits for this place. Did he have Simon's dad in his back pocket? Lori shuddered at the thought.

Though Dell Wingate was in Atlanta far more than

in his native Pine Bluff, Lori had always respected their assemblyman. The Wingates were a case study in superior genetics. Dell was open, affable and handsome. She also believed he held their district's best interests at heart. Would he have helped a scumbag like Coulter set up shop in their own backyard?

She followed the waving hands of a pimply-faced teenager in a yellow safety vest. She and Lena didn't speak as they bumped across a field mowed down to be the parking area. He waved her into a spot beside a pickup truck so dented and rusted Lori feared for her car's doors and quarter panels. Reaching across, she held on to her sister's arm to keep her in place until another car slid into the spot on the driver's side. "Hold up. Let's let them all get out first."

Lena huffed, but waited. When the coast was clear, they opened their doors cautiously, careful not to touch the vehicles wedged in tight. Lori didn't exactly drag her feet as they headed toward the entry, but she did hang back. Years of training had her on high alert, scanning the crowd, the single points of entrance and egress, and eyeballing the uniformed staff manning the gate.

Lena raced ahead toward the plywood outbuilding marked Ticket Office, but Lori walked slowly, checking out the patrons who'd chosen to spend their Saturday afternoon and a chunk of their paychecks on this, of all things.

Lori purchased their tickets, all the while resenting the thought of her hard-earned money going to line the pockets of a guy who was reportedly already a millionaire. She followed her sister to the turnstile inside where arrows pointed them in about four different directions. None of the offerings remotely appealed to Lori.

"I don't suppose we can start with the turtles?" she asked Lena, indicating one of the arrows.

The younger girl smiled but nodded to another arrow. "I'm pretty sure Jas said something about boa constrictors being the least gross of all the snakes."

Lori hiked her purse high on her shoulder and followed when Lena set off in the indicated direction. "How do you think she figures they are the least gross?"

Lena didn't glance back when she shrugged. "They swallow things whole, right? No biting?"

"I have no earthly idea," Lori replied honestly. "I think maybe they bite, but they aren't venomous. They paralyze their prey and just…squeeze." She blew out a breath when the path widened to what appeared to be some kind of viewing area. "I don't think I want to know."

Lena giggled when an enclosure covered in fine wire mesh came into view. "I don't either."

"Maybe no one will notice if we look away," Lori whispered. They moved to the back of the group of people knotted at the rail and peering into the massive cage.

Lori's heart rate kicked up a few notches when she saw the slow slide of a thick, scaly creature moving along the base of the enclosure. "This can't be safe," she muttered.

Lena snorted a laugh but took a step back, nearly crushing Lori's big toe in the process. "He can't un-latch the gate thingy," she answered. "No thumbs, remember?"

A few more people came up behind them, and the two of them sank deeper into the back of the crowd, eyeing the enclosure warily. Nearby, Lori heard a woman say something to her companion about it being nearly feeding time, and she shuddered when her own ghoulish stomach gave a loud rumble.

Then a young man wearing khaki pants and a safari-style shirt with an interlocking-*R* logo on the patch pocket stepped out of a hidden doorway at the back of the enclosure. The short sleeves of his uni-form shirt did nothing to hide the artwork on his arms. Tattoos of serpents slithered out from under the cotton to wind around his forearms. When he lifted a five-gallon pail by the handle, Lori caught a glimpse of a flat-eyed snake head inked into the back of his hand.

She tore her gaze away from those mesmerizing tats to look up at the guy's face. He was young—nineteen, tops. The scruffy beard he was cultivating did him no favors in the looks department, but the even white smile he flashed at the crowd more than made up for his appearance.

"Oh, my God," the sisters said in unison.

"That's him, isn't it?" When Lena didn't answer, Lori glanced over and saw her sister staring at some-one in the front row of spectators. "What? What's wrong?"

Lena nodded to the rail, and Lori saw a petite dark-haired girl grinning and waving to the young man inside the cage. "Is that Jasmine?"

Lena swallowed hard and nodded emphatically.

Lori tracked the guy she presumed to be Rick. He made his way around the enclosure with practiced ease. When he launched into a fairly generic-sounding spiel about boa constrictors, their natural habitats and the characteristics unique to the species, she tuned out. Lifting her gaze, she caught sight of another, smaller snake wound around the branch of one of the enclosure's trees and wondered if this was the cage Bella Nunes had been locked in, or if Coulter chose to use more-venomous creatures to terrorize his guests.

Forcing herself to focus on the task at hand, she leaned closer to her sister and whispered, "Did she say she was going to be here today? Is that why we came?"

Lena's narrow shoulders jerked up and down, but she shook her head. "She said she was doing something with her mom."

Lori was about to launch into a round of reassuring comments when her sister whirled to face her. "Can we go now?"

It was on the tip of her tongue to remind Lena she'd paid fifteen dollars a ticket to get them through the gate merely five minutes ago, but the desperation written all over her sister's face was enough to discount the price of admission.

"Yep." Wrapping her arm around Lena's shoulders,

she nodded to the path leading back to the front gate. "Come on. Let's get out of here."

They'd almost made it back to the entrance when Lena said sullenly, "He's not even cute in person."

Lori could see why the guy would appeal to a young woman looking for a walk on the wild side. She wouldn't defend Jasmine's questionable taste in guys, so she said the only thing a real sister could say. "No, definitely not."

Lena veered toward the small building marked Restrooms. "I'll only be a minute," she promised, darting toward the ladies' room. Lori could have used a pit stop herself, but something in the way Lena moved said her sister needed a minute alone, so she held back.

Leaning against a block wall, Lori watched a steady trickle of people come and go. It was by no means a Six Flags crowd, but for a patch of nothing in the middle of nowhere, she had to admit old Sammy was doing a steady business on a sunny Saturday afternoon.

Her gaze strayed to the small thatched roof of a kiosk where a young girl stood selling souvenirs. There was something familiar about the girl, but the niggling sensation wasn't unusual. Most of the families in rural Masters County came to Pine Bluff to do their banking and shopping. It was possible she'd been seeing the girl around town for years without truly noticing her.

Lori's gaze drifted away, but she jerked her attention back when she realized exactly where she'd seen the girl. She pulled out her phone and checked the notification she'd saved. Straightening away from the building, she locked in on the girl and whispered, "Kaylin Bowers."

Instinctively, she reached for her belt, forgetting she was off duty. Her trusty Glock was in her purse, but drawing a weapon in a crowded place was not a good idea. She needed to get a better look at the girl. Lori took two steps toward the small souvenir stand. Kaylin didn't seem to be there under duress. As a matter of fact, she was smiling. She was about to approach the girl when her sister came out of nowhere to grab her arm and spin her toward the exit.

"Come on. I want to go," Lena insisted.

"Okay, but, honey—" Lori twisted to look back over her shoulder to be sure her eyes weren't deceiving her.

"Now, Lori, please?" Lena wheedled.

Lori planted her feet and looked back at the souvenir stand. Kaylin smiled wide as she was relieved from souvenir duty by another young man with a crisp khaki shirt.

"Well, damn," Lori muttered to herself. "Everyone does want to work here."

"Can we go?" Lena repeated. "I want to get out of here."

Judging by the girl's happy demeanor, Kaylin had obviously left home of her own free will. If she approached, she might scare her off. Aware that her own teenage sister was watching, Lori backed away a step. Lena would not appreciate Lori drawing too much attention to them, particularly when she was so desperate to leave without Jasmine knowing they'd seen her. The best thing she could do was to call in the sighting and let the officer on duty handle things.

"Okay, but I need to make a call."

They pushed their way through the exit, and Lena took off across the rutted field. Lori pulled her phone from her purse and speed-dialed the office. "Mike? Listen, I'm out of uniform and with my sister, but can you saddle up and make your way over to the Reptile Rendezvous?" She paused when they reached her car, and she looked back at the entrance. "Yeah. Reptile Rendezvous. Alert the fellas over at Prescott County. I've spotted Kaylin Bowers selling souvenirs on Samuel Coulter's property."

Chapter Six

Simon's Saturday started going downhill late Friday afternoon, which had to be some kind of record. He'd received a call from Samuel Coulter as he was packing up his briefcase.

"I've shipped a package to your office overnight express. It's valuable. I need you to be there to sign for it," Coulter announced without preamble.

Taken aback by the man's audacity, Simon answered with only a murmured "Tomorrow is Saturday."

"I am aware, but I'm in Florida to do some, uh, fishing." Coulter paused. "I was informed the merchandise I ordered was available for immediate shipment, so I asked them to direct it your way."

"I'm not in the habit of receiving packages of unknown origin or packages addressed to persons other than myself," Simon informed him.

"A good policy in general, but I am your client. I recall a rather hefty retainer tacked onto our agreement for billable hours." The other man chuckled, and Simon stiffened. "I'm sure the retainer must cover signatory services."

"Why not send it to your own business?"

"I can't trust some hourly knucklehead with anything truly important. I only pay them a dollar over minimum wage. This box is valuable. I'd hate for it to go astray."

"I can't accept delivery of anything illegal."

"Then I suggest, for your own comfort, you stop asking questions and don't try to open my box."

With that, his client had hung up. Simon could only assume the man had silenced his phone, since repeated attempts to call him back went unanswered.

And so, he'd gone into the office on Saturday morning. While he was waiting, he called his grandfather. "Hey, do I have the pleasure of speaking to the almost honorable Wendell Wingate?" he asked when the older man answered.

"There are some who'd argue the 'almost' should apply even if I am elected," Wendell answered with a chortle.

"*When* you are elected," Simon corrected. "I think most of us would be okay with being called almost honorable. Beats being called a slimy snake handler."

The old man guffawed. "I take it your new client isn't winning any popularity contests?"

"Not with the local law enforcement," Simon answered, a wry smile twisting his lips when he pictured Lori Cabrera squaring off with him at the Daisy Drive-In. "I have to admit, I'm not particularly a fan either."

"Well, you don't have to befriend the man. You only have to be his lawyer," his grandfather reminded him.

"Right." Simon rocked back in the enormous

leather chair the old man had sat in and studied the shelves of leather-bound volumes behind the desk. "Which is why I'm at the office on a Saturday morning. Coulter had a package shipped to our offices. Says it's valuable and will require a signature."

In an instant, his grandfather's jovial bonhomie disappeared. Wendell was all business when he asked, "Did he say what the package contained?"

"He did not give specifics, and I did not ask for them," Simon replied, skimming over the gilt-lettered spines of decades-old law books.

When he was a kid, he'd often wondered if they were for show. If maybe those expensive cordovan covers were simply a shell for blank pages, or perhaps they were hollowed-out hidey-holes. His first foray into a law library left him feeling overwhelmed and vaguely disappointed. Though he'd slogged through all three years of law school, he graduated with a new understanding of why his father had chosen politics over the practice of law.

"Good," Wendell grunted, interrupting his wandering thoughts. "Now, here's what I want you to do. Call Dora and bribe her to come in and witness you signing for this package. Take photos of the box from all different angles to show no one has tampered with it in any way. Have Dora email the photos to you and copy the client. The delivery driver will have a time stamp, and you'll have one too. When Coulter comes to collect the package, I want you to take pictures of your own to show the package was intact when he took receipt."

Simon sat up straight, the back of the leather chair snapping back into place with a thunk. "Isn't that overkill?"

"Better too much caution than too little," his grandfather admonished. "What's the first thing you learn in law school? Either bury the facts, or bury them *in* facts. Depends which side you're on."

"I'm starting to wonder myself," Simon muttered.

"You're on your side," Wendell replied stubbornly. "Now, you listen to me. I worked those backwoods my entire life. There are people there who are fine, upstanding citizens. Then there are those who should live under a fallen log." Simon snorted, but Wendell plowed ahead, his tenor becoming more strident with each word. "You think you're dealing with a bunch of banjo-playing hillbillies out there. You think you're smarter than they are with your diplomas and tailored suits, but the biggest mistake you can make is thinking they can't outmaneuver you. There are no shadows deeper than those cast in the woods, and Coulter's kind have been creeping through them their whole lives."

"Or slithering," Simon countered, unable to resist putting up at least a token resistance to the truths his grandfather was doling out.

"As the case may be. Make no mistake—his type of man doesn't flourish in sunlight."

"How did you do this? How could you spend your whole life defending people who are up to no good?"

Wendell paused long enough for regret to pool in Simon's gut. An apology poised on the tip of his tongue, he rested his forehead on the heel of his palm. "Granddad—"

"Believe it or not, it wasn't always this bad," Wendell said, a wistful note entering his tone. "Sure, I had moonshiners and the usual run-of-the-mill ruffians to deal with. The worst were actually the men who thought it was okay to knock their wives around. I didn't have much stomach for defending them."

"I don't blame you."

"Of course, there were some ugly incidents between the whites and the blacks. Most of the time it came down to some white boys inciting trouble, then twisting things around until they could press charges against the people of color, so I actually got to defend a passel of those cases. Won a few of them too, though not as many as I should have. Depended on the judge and jury."

Simon rubbed his eyes with his thumb and forefinger. He'd hardly slept the previous night, and listening to his grandfather talk about all the tough choices he'd had to make over the years made him feel whiny for complaining about this one guy.

"Granddad, I'm—"

Wendell cut him off. "It's not an easy job, Simon, but it's a necessary one." His voice warmed and gentled. "Focus on the good you'll do."

"Hard to do when I haven't done much more than get people out of speeding tickets. And defend scumbags so I can keep the lights on," he added.

"It's enough for now. You're not building your life's work there," Wendell reminded him.

"I could ruin yours," Simon answered gloomily.

"Nah. Anyone can draw up a will on a computer these days. We're mainly there to read things through and provide reassurance. You need this time to figure out what your path is going to be." He paused, and Simon braced himself for further discussion about the stumbles he'd already made on that path, but his grandfather surprised him by reverting back to Coulter.

"I assume you did some research on this guy before you took him on?"

"Of course I did." Simon tried to squelch the defensiveness in his tone, but wasn't entirely successful.

"Give me a rough sketch."

"Born in Miami. Solidly middle-class upbringing. Went to Florida State for a couple of years, but dropped out when he discovered the stock market," Simon reported dutifully. "Made a pile of money trading online. I think he was a millionaire before he turned twenty-five."

His grandfather let loose with a low whistle. "Impressive."

Simon scowled. Something in him didn't want Wendell to be impressed by the likes of Samuel Coulter. "Anyway, started running with a bunch of South Florida high rollers. Some fairly sketchy, others legit. Soon, the company he was keeping and the money he was making drew the attention of the Feds."

"Charges?"

Simon shook his head, though he knew his grandfather couldn't see him. "Investigations, insinuations, but nothing concrete. Coulter scaled back on his trading and turned to his other hobby."

"The snake thing," Wendell concluded.

"Started as a collector, but likes to refer to himself as a naturalist, or a conservationist," Simon reported dryly.

"And the move from Florida to Georgia? That's a hell of a change in social scenery."

"I'm not entirely clear on the ins and outs of it all, but he claims he was feeling hemmed in by the city. I think he got sideways with the Florida Fish and Wildlife Conservation Commission on something and wanted to be somewhere where people might not be paying close attention."

"If he moved to a small town for anonymity, he made a grave miscalculation," Wendell said with a chuckle.

Simon forced a laugh himself. "No kidding."

Tired of talking about Coulter, and hoping to avoid any rehashing of the mistakes that had landed him in Pine Bluff, he switched the subject to his attempt at making life in town more palatable.

"I'm hosting a cookout at your place, and Marlee Masters is supposed to come," he said gruffly. "I'm going to offer to take some of the Timber Masters business back from her, since she has her plate full."

Wendell chuckled. "That's my boy. Generous to a fault."

"I've also been trying to make nice with the folks over at the municipal building. I invited Harrison Hayes, Sheriff Kinsella and the deputies."

"Smart move. They're good people."

"Hayes and Kinsella seem to be okay with me, but Deputy Cabrera hates my guts."

"Lori?" Wendell sounded genuinely surprised. "I doubt she does."

"She thinks I should go crawl under a log with my client."

Wendell chuckled. "Yeah, well, she always has had a strictly defined line between right and wrong. If she thinks you've crossed it, she'll make you work to get back on her good side."

"You're speaking from experience," he observed.

"I got a few of her perps off the hook, so I wasn't on her list of favorite people for a while there."

Unable to resist, Simon asked, "How'd you get back on there? She speaks pretty highly of you now."

"I helped her aunt once. Miss Anita's husband died of cancer a few years after they signed a pickle of a rent-to-own agreement on a house. The whole setup was illegal, but the owner never figured on an immigrant being brave enough to call him out. I got the judge to order a settlement and rendered the property paid in full."

"Oh, so all I have to do is pull a rabbit out of my hat," Simon said wryly.

"She's a tough cookie. And a smart one. Anita left her house to Lori in her will."

"Her will?"

"Car accident. Both Anita and Lori's father, Mateo, were killed. Been over a year, but the family is still reeling. They had a restaurant in town, but it was all too much for Sophia, Lori's mother, to keep going. There was some life insurance money, so she closed the business and has been focused on her children."

"I'm sorry to hear that," Simon replied, ingrained manners kicking in.

"It's been a rough couple of years for Lori. Losing Jeff Masters, then her father and aunt. The house was a nice gesture on Anita's part, but I don't believe Lori's mother has taken kindly to her moving out of the family home."

Simon's curiosity was piqued on several levels, but he went for the easiest question first. "Why not?"

"I'm told it's a cultural thing," Wendell explained. "Young women are expected to live at home with their parents until they marry."

"She served in the army," Simon said with a perplexed laugh.

"Doesn't count," Wendell replied.

"Huh. Well, okay," he said, giving up on that line of questioning for one he found more intriguing. "You said something about Jeff Masters?"

"Well, I wasn't aware of it at the time, but it turns out that Lori and Jeff were…involved at the time of his death. Naturally, she was quite upset when we believed he committed suicide, but when it became apparent it was murder… Well, I think the events of the past couple of years have shaken her confidence."

Simon couldn't contain the short laugh that escaped him. If this was Lori feeling shaky, she must have been formidable in the days before life threw all that grief at her.

"Are you hopin' to impress our lovely young deputy at this cookout?"

He should have seen the sneak attack coming, but he never did. He laughed, the sound bursting out of him so abruptly, he realized he couldn't remember the last time he'd done it. Recovering quickly, he took a mental step back and parried the question.

"I'm simply hoping to get off one list and onto the other."

The evasion came so naturally to him, Simon wondered if he might have spent too much time in rooms filled with politicians. Either way, he needed to end this call and get his plea in with Dora if he wanted to have someone witness the delivery of Samuel Coulter's mystery package.

"I'd better go, Granddad. I need to catch Dora and see what her price will be."

"Oh, she's an easy one. Cash money. Tell her you'll pay her triple time, and she'll hightail it right on over. She lives to spoil those grandbabies of hers, and the eldest has his heart set on a trip down to Disney."

"Money it is," Simon agreed.

"And don't make Lori mad. The woman carries and she's a crack shot."

"Talk to you again soon, Granddad."

"Okay, and be sure to cover your flank." His grandfather's affectionate laugh was a balm. Unfortunately, the comfort the call provided didn't last long.

HE'D STARTED THE day by paying a small fortune to secure a witness to his taking possession of a box full of what he suspected may be contraband snakes. Once the job was done, all he wanted to do was go home and take the second shower. Unfortunately, he received an irate phone call from his client telling him the deputy Simon hadn't been able to get out of his mind had staged a one-woman raid on his client's property.

Simon's nostrils flared. He tried to control the irritation bubbling inside him. One Saturday. All he wanted was one Saturday to hang out with some people and possibly lay the groundwork for friendlier relations between himself and some of his new colleagues and neighbors.

But no. He'd spent hours chasing down enough information to satisfy his client. Thankfully, Coulter wasn't in any real trouble this time. He might get some flak for his manager's suspect hiring practices, but the fourteen-year-old runaway they'd picked up at the Reptile Rendezvous admitted to having used a fake ID to get the job.

Her "boyfriend," one of the half-dozen scruffy young guys Coulter had hired to work the exhibitions, claimed he had no idea Kaylin Bowers was underage. Fortunately for young Justin, he was only seventeen. The combination of his age and the evidence of Kaylin misrepresenting her age on social media had kept the boy out of any further legal trouble, but the unwelcome spotlight the girl's recovery had shone on Coulter had likely cost the kid his job.

His client was somehow involved in yet another girl-in-peril situation, and it didn't sit well with Simon.

Neither did the discovery that Lori Cabrera had been the one who'd spotted the missing girl working at the Reptile Rendezvous. What business did she have hanging around his client's property? She'd said she was spending the day with her sister. Had she gone there to check on the guy she said her sister's friend was into? Or had she been fishing for something bigger to hook his client?

Simon vented his frustration by scooping the contents of pint containers of deli-prepared potato salad out with a spoon and thwacking the globs into the festively patterned melamine serving bowls his grandfather's supposedly retired housekeeper insisted he use for cookouts with "company."

He'd made the mistake of asking Miss Delia where she stashed his grandfather's grilling supplies. She'd shown up at his door an hour earlier and marched through the kitchen pulling plates, platters, bowls and utensils from cabinets and drawers, all the while spewing a stream of instructions Simon hadn't had a chance in hell of remembering.

She'd smirked when she saw he'd bought both mustard and mayonnaise varieties of potato salad, but said nothing. He'd bought both because he had no idea what people around here preferred, but Simon had no doubt whatsoever there'd be strong opinions on the matter. There seemed to be strong opinions on about everything in Pine Bluff, large and small. Delia had offered no clues. She'd simply laid everything out on the kitchen counter, told him she and her husband would be back in time for kickoff, then left with a pat on the cheek.

Now he stood seething in the kitchen, half-afraid he might cross-examine Lourdes Cabrera about her motives if she dared to show up. He was trying to make the best of his time here in Purgatory Bluff, damn it. The woman seemed determined to take his client down, and here he was, torn between forcing her to take a step back and wanting to make a move on her. He needed to get a grip.

The doorbell rang and he checked his watch. It was only five o'clock. His first guest was thirty minutes early, and he hadn't even had time to change. Hurrying to the front door, he wiped his sticky hands on his gym shorts and hoped whoever it was had come prepared to help.

When he sneaked a peek through the sidelight window, he drew up short. Lori stood on his porch wearing oven mitts and carrying a large cast-iron pot.

She must have caught him peeking, because she called through the closed door. "Hurry. This thing weighs a ton."

He pulled open the door. The percolating bubbles of anger had carried him through the afternoon, but fizzled out the second he saw her. Her thick coffee-colored hair was caught up in a big messy bun on top of her head. Tendrils escaped at her temples. He itched to touch one, but curled his fingers into his palm to keep from acting on the impulse. Staring into her wide brown eyes, he could barely contain his pleasure at seeing her. "You made it."

"Hi. Yes. I'm early, but I brought baked beans, and I wanted the chance to talk to you alone."

He swung the door open wide and gestured for her to enter. "I'm not quite set up yet, but come on in."

He caught the scent of a light floral perfume as she passed him. She wore olive green cargo shorts. They probably wouldn't have been as sexy on anybody else but appeared to have been made with Lori in mind. Her lush curves stretched the fabric taut, but not too tight. A formfitting gray T-shirt with a deep V-neck and the University of Georgia's trademark *G* completed the look.

Afraid he'd been caught ogling the lucky consonant, he waved a hand toward the back of the house. "Come on back to the kitchen." Extending his hands, he nodded to the heavy-looking pot she held. "Here. Let me take that."

She pulled the pot closer to her. "I better hang on to it. It's hot from the oven."

He led the way to the kitchen. She marched directly to Delia's six-burner stove and plunked the cast-iron pot down on the grate. "Beautiful kitchen," she said, her face aglow with admiration.

"It was a bribe."

She glanced at him in surprise. "A bribe?"

Simon simply shrugged. "Miss Delia wanted to retire about a year after my grandma passed, but Wendell wasn't quite ready to take on the bachelor life. She said she couldn't go on working in such an outdated kitchen, so he had this built for her."

Lori turned in a slow, appraising circle. "It's gorgeous. I love the way it opens out onto the patio."

"I think Delia only sticks around because her kitchen at home isn't up to snuff now."

"Does she cook for you?"

He shook his head. "No. Once Wendell left, she abdicated. She comes by every now and again to make sure I'm putting the forks in the right slot." Simon watched with keen interest when Lori bent to adjust the gas flame to burn low and steady underneath the pot.

"Wow." She ran a hand over one of the heavy grates. "My mother would kill to have this stove."

Simon felt a pang of sadness when he recalled Wendell's story about the family restaurant, but didn't want to let on they'd been talking about her, so he stuck to the facts. "Miss Delia has good taste in almost everything."

Lori stepped away from the range and slid the other oven mitt from her hand. She placed the cartoon twosome on the counter and stepped back to have a better look around. "Almost everything?"

"Well, we've always found her loyalty to my grandfather suspect."

Lori laughed, and the sound punched him right in the gut. He braced himself for impact, but realized there was no way on earth a man could be prepared for her unguarded smile. His wits scattered, he switched straight into babble mode. "I didn't think you were coming."

"I wasn't sure if I would," she replied with her usual candor. Crossing her arms over the *G* emblem, she leaned back against the counter and studied him through narrowed eyes. "I assume you spoke to your client today," she said, her demeanor a shade shy of confrontational.

"I have several clients, but if you are referring to Mr. Coulter, yes, I have," he retorted.

She rolled her eyes. "Let's shoot straight, okay?"

The agitation Simon tamped down came roaring back to life. "I always do, whether you choose to believe me or not." Needing to keep busy, he moved back to the counter lined with platters and bowls and continued transferring potato salad from the deli container to the approved serving bowl. He then peeled the lid off a container of mustard potato salad. "Why were you there?" he asked as he started whacking spoonfuls into another bowl.

"I went because my sister asked me to take her to the refuge." She moved to stand beside him and began checking the labels on the containers stacked there. "How many people are you expecting?" she asked, clearly amused by his propensity to overshop.

"I wasn't sure what to get, so I bought a little of everything. Plus, I think word has spread."

Lori reached for one of the serving bowls. "It always does around here."

He watched out of the corner of his eye as she pried the lid off a container of three-bean salad and dumped it into the bowl.

"One of Lena's friends is into a guy who works at Coulter's place."

"You mentioned something about that when we talked the other day."

"She was curious. Lena was, I mean. She wanted to get a look at the guy her best friend has essentially dumped her for."

He turned to look at her, concern furrowing his brow. "You said she was only sixteen. Is she dating the guy?"

Lori shrugged. "It sounds more like chasing than dating, but who knows. Kids can be so secretive at that age."

His mouth drew into a tight line. She wasn't wrong in that assessment. Few kids were immune to teenage rebellion. He himself had had some exploits that would have made Dell tear his expertly barbered hair out if he'd caught wind of them. "Yes. They can."

She went to work on the macaroni salad next, her head bent in concentration. "I didn't go there looking for Kaylin Bowers, and I want you to hear me when I say I wasn't looking for a reason to harass your client."

"I hear you, but I got a call all the same." He grabbed two of the bowls he'd filled and made his way to the refrigerator.

Lori took hold of hers and followed. "I'm sorry if I caused you trouble, but I was only doing my job. If I'd seen her at the Daisy or in the Piggly Wiggly, I would've done the exact same thing."

"Understood. I hope the young lady is okay," he said tersely.

When their gazes met, he let his shoulders sag as he breathed out some of the frustration that seemed to be part and parcel of doing business with Samuel Coulter. Then he shook himself. He definitely didn't want to think about parcels. God, Lori's head would probably explode if she found out he'd signed for a mystery box for Coulter.

Shaking it off, he gave her a wan smile. "Can we... change the subject?"

"Okay," she agreed readily. "What's the saying about the evils of the day being enough?"

Simon smiled. "'Sufficient unto the day is the evil thereof.'"

"Exactly."

They shared a smile, and for the first time since she'd crossed his threshold, Simon wished he'd had the time to change out of his gym shorts. "I, uh... Do you mind entertaining yourself while I change?"

Lori's smile widened and her cheeks colored when she gave him a quick once-over. "Oh, sure, but you look fine." The color staining her cheeks deepened. "I mean, it's a football game."

He plucked at the front of the plain charcoal T-shirt he wore. "Thanks, but I need to support the home team. Wouldn't want people thinking I'm pulling for the other guys."

She laughed and moved to the counter. "The other team is gonna need all the help it can get," she said, gathering the discarded deli containers. Walking them over to the stainless-steel trash can, she made a show of stepping on the pedal to lift the lid. "And this one time, I'll even help you bury evidence, Counselor."

Chapter Seven

Something about being left alone inside Simon Wingate's personal space felt decadent. Lori stood in the kitchen letting her gaze travel along the veins in the marble countertops. She caught a glimpse of her reflection in a glass-front cabinet and lifted a hand to her hair. She felt slightly undone by her surroundings. She could only dream of having a house this big and comfortable. She was both enraptured and discomfited.

The stylish surroundings weren't what was making her feel antsy now. Or the feeling she didn't belong there. She was used to not quite belonging. It was Simon. She was more susceptible to the man than she wanted to be. Which meant she needed to tread carefully around him.

She wandered down the hall to the large family room she'd spotted on her way in. An enormous, comfortable-looking sectional dominated the space. A flat-screen television that appeared to have been selected for its ability to match the size of the couch hung on the wall above a gas log fireplace. The room was filled with books, knickknacks and family photos.

They couldn't be Simon's. If he had been the one to decorate this room, she would lay odds that the studio shot of the freckle-faced, mildly gap-toothed Cub Scout sitting front and center on the middle shelf would have been stashed in the deepest drawer he could find.

She was drawn to it like a beacon.

How could a boy who'd sworn the Scout's oath grow up to be a man who defended a suspected man like Samuel Coulter?

Swallowing her distaste, she studied the photo for hints of what this innocent, winsome Simon would become. His hair had darkened only a shade or two. His eyes sparkled with the same mischievous gleam he'd inherited from his grandfather.

Annoyed, she placed the photo carefully back on the shelf and walked away. She spotted multiple shots of Simon's father, Dell. The second Wendell Wingate, she thought to herself, was a man made for public life. He was a handsome man, but his looks skewed more toward Wendell's affable country gentleman than Simon's cool, urbane facade. He was clean-cut, where his son leaned toward polished.

Lori could only conclude Simon inherited his sheen from his mother. She reached for one of the posed family photographs that showed Bettina Wingate to be the epitome of all-American blonde beauty. She had a sort of old Hollywood glamour. Like Grace Kelly dressed up as a sweet Georgia peach of a girl next door. Her smile was wide and winning, like her son's, but she gleamed with a fine coat of gloss.

She was startled from her reverie by the sound of Simon clearing his throat. Lori quickly set the photograph back in its spot and flashed him a sheepish smile. "Sorry. I was snooping."

His amused smile grew into an unabashed grin. "You're a cop—you could probably classify your snooping as detective work, and no one would argue any different."

"Should I be investigating your family?" she asked, raising a challenging eyebrow.

Simon laughed and pulled his hands from the pockets of his jeans. "Snoop away. My dad has held some form of elected office nearly my whole life. If the press hasn't managed to unearth any dirt vile enough to damage the family reputation, I'm feeling pretty confident there isn't any to be had."

"What you see is what you get?"

She tried to make the question sound casual, but the way her heart beat a staccato when she noticed the way his damp hair curled where it brushed the collar of his red-and-black-striped polo made her feel the opposite of cool. The Georgia Bulldog embroidered over one nicely outlined pec gave her an I-see-what-you're-doing stare, but she refused to be intimidated by a mascot.

Lori studied him closely. "How about you? Is politics your plan too?"

Without hesitating, he nodded. "My dad plans to run for the Senate when Senator Riley's term is up. I may throw my hat in the ring for his seat in the Georgia General Assembly."

Despite herself, Lori was surprised by the bomb he'd dropped into the conversation oh so casually. "Wait—Senator Blake Riley?"

He nodded and her heart kicked up at the thought of it. Blake Riley had served in the Senate for longer than anyone cared to remember. He was a jerk. A camera-hamming bigot. Lori found it odd for someone who lived to draw attention to himself to head quietly into retirement, but she wasn't about to complain.

"Your dad is running for the US Senate?"

Simon's mouth curved up on one side. He held a finger to his lips. "That's a state secret. And no one is beating down the door asking me to run for anything."

She noticed Simon's self-deprecating drawl deepened when he was doling out glib bits of unvarnished truth. The knowledge did something to Lori's insides. Something she wasn't sure she liked. With every slow, soft-spoken syllable, her resolve to keep her distance from this man softened and stretched like taffy pulled on a hot summer day.

"What can I get you to drink?" he asked, jerking her out of her thoughts.

"Anything's fine," she replied.

"I can offer you water or, uh, water," he said with a shrug. "Hayes said he'd be bringing the beverages."

"How about water?"

"Be right back."

She didn't want to have sticky-taffy feelings for Simon Wingate. Liking him would only complicate things. He had plans for moving up and out of Pine Bluff. She had a family who needed her to stay grounded. Or get regrounded. More than anything, Lori wished she could be the woman she was two years ago. Someone strong, confident that she could hurdle any obstacle thrown at her. And she had. She'd steered her family through the loss of her father and aunt. She'd helped her mother recalibrate her life as a widow and stepped into the void her father had left as best she could.

But then Jeff Masters killed himself, and her belief in her ability to be the person her loved ones needed was shaken to the core. He'd left no note. There'd been no hint of dissatisfaction. She'd been as shocked as the Masters family. But she wasn't a part of the family. Most people hadn't even known they were dating, so how could she explain how deeply she grieved his loss? The discovery that Jeff had been coerced into pulling that trigger was just one more blow to her already shaky self-assurance.

Lori stared at the Wingate family portrait. Simon would marry a woman like his mother, composed and serene. A woman with a heaping helping of confidence and free of messy complications. If Ben Kinsella hadn't snatched up Marlee Masters the minute she sauntered back into town, Lori would've laid odds that Marlee and Simon would be planning a trip down the aisle by now. Surely the thought had crossed Henry Masters's and Wendell Wingate's minds.

Simon returned with two bottles of water, a bag of chips and a bowl filled with bright red salsa. "Dig in." He paused, frowning at his offering. "I didn't make it. They have containers of it in the refrigerated case. The cashier, Tina? She said it was locally made."

Lori's smile started to unfurl. "Was it called Bonita Anita?"

Simon set the bowl on the table in front of her. "Yes. Have you tried it? It's so good."

The smile widened to a grin. "Yes, I have. My mother makes it."

"Are you kidding me? I'm totally hooked on the stuff."

Lori's limbs loosened. She beamed with familial pride. "I'll be sure to pass your compliments along." She inclined her head. "And thank you for your patronage."

He shook his head in wonder. "Your mother makes it? I've been eating it nonstop since I moved here. It's the best thing about this whole town."

Torn between flattery and insult, Lori stared at him. "Wow. Thanks for the rousing endorsement."

He opened his mouth to correct himself, then gave up with a shrug. "Foodwise, I mean."

Tickled by his stubborn refusal to show the town any love, she unleashed the laugh she'd been holding back. "Poor city mouse, stuck out here with us country bumpkins. My aunt used to have a restaurant. This was a family recipe."

Rather than the smart reply she'd expected, Simon stared at her. This time, there was no derision in his gaze, only compassion. Which meant he knew about her father and her aunt. Talk about a conversation killer. She could feel the blush creeping up from her chest. Lord, if she kept blushing beet red every time he looked at her, he would think she was an actual redneck.

"No one here but us rubes," she whispered.

"Wendell told me not to make you mad. He says you carry."

"I do."

"I heard you're quite the shot."

"I am, but they don't let me fire at live targets," she replied, unable to keep her pride hidden away like the compact Glock she carried when off duty.

"I'm torn between being impressed and terrified."

"Both will do." She narrowed her eyes. "Did you want a demonstration or something?"

A knock made them both jump, and the front door hinges squeaked a warning.

"Hello? Simon?" Dora called out, letting herself in. "I made Rotel dip," she announced, carrying in a slow cooker with its cord dangling right past the doorway to the foyer. "I chopped up some of those canned tamales and tossed them in. I figured if your granddad liked—" She backpedaled, craning her neck when she spotted them in the family room. "Hey, Lori." Dora's smile was friendly, but something sharp and speculative gleamed in her eyes. "You made it after all."

Simon rushed across the room to relieve Dora of her burden. "I told you I invited everyone." He divided a look between Dora and Lori, then ducked his head. "I'll just take this to the kitchen."

Dora watched him hurry down the hall, then took a giant, showy side step into the family room, where Lori sat frozen. "I'm so glad you're here. I swear, Simon's been living like a seventy-year-old bachelor since he came to town."

For some reason, Lori felt compelled to set the record straight. "Oh, no, I, uh—"

"Hush. He needs something more pleasant than work to think about. Particularly with old Cottonmouth Coulter treating him like he's some kind of errand boy."

"Errand boy?" Lori started to rise.

"Not important," Dora said with a dismissive wave. "I'll go get my dip set up so it stays warm and send Simon back in here. You stay put."

The woman click-clacked down the hall in a pair of red leather mules with giant *G*s emblazoned across the insteps.

Rather than staying out as ordered, Lori paced. The gleam in Dora's eye, combined with the heat in Simon's, made her feel antsy. Like her skin was too tight. Shaking out her hands, she prowled the space while her lizard brain debated between fight or flight.

A clatter arose from the kitchen, followed by Dora's raised voice ordering Simon from the room. Then it struck her. She didn't trust herself to be alone with him. If they were left alone, God only knew what she might ask him.

Are you Coulter's errand boy?

What kind of errands?
Do you like me?
Are you planning to stay here in Pine Bluff?
Do you want to kiss me?
Why couldn't I want to kiss Hayes instead of you?

The thoughts ping-ponged around in her head. Scared she'd open her mouth and one might pop out, she decided to take the coward's way out. Abandoning her water, she skirted the end of the sectional and headed for the hall, her sights set on the front door.

She almost made it.

One step into the hall and she collided with Simon so hard her bun wobbled. He grasped both of her arms to steady her.

"Whoa, there." He exhaled and planted his feet wide, absorbing the impact with a chuckle. "Where are you headed in such a hurry?"

Mortified, Lori tried to pretend her mouth had not almost come in contact with the Georgia Bulldog appliquéd to his shirt. A flash fire of a blush overheated her face. She tipped her head back, and the weight of her hair pulled at her scalp. She wished she could say the sensation was unpleasant, but when a girl found herself wrapped up in Simon Wingate's arms…

Her lips parted and she scrambled for an excuse to leave. Any excuse. Then his gaze dropped to her mouth and any words she might have conjured dried to dust. He tilted his head to the side and she automatically did the same. She couldn't help it. He was going to kiss her. And she was going to let him, because how could she not?

He dipped his head and—

The doorbell rang.

The courtesy had been perfunctory at best. She'd barely had time to register the sound when the door swung wide and Marlee Masters hollered, "Go, Dawgs…"

"Doesn't anyone wait to come in around here?" Simon muttered.

Lori stepped back, her gaze locked on Marlee. To her credit, her friend swapped her stunned expression with a blazing smile in the blink of an eye. "I have a peach cobbler!" she said in lieu of a response.

Bless her heart, Marlee stood there in the doorway, trying to take up all the room a lanky blonde holding a casserole dish possibly could. Lori could see Ben coming up behind her. Thankfully, he looked to be absorbed in helping Henry Masters navigate the shallow front steps with his walker.

Lori took another step back, plunging her hands into the pockets of her shorts. She fingered her car keys like a talisman capable of warding off hot attorneys of questionable morals.

"I have to go," she announced abruptly.

"What?" Simon's eyebrows drew together, and a deep but not unattractive furrow appeared.

Lori sidled past him as if he were radioactive, then came face-to-face with Marlee. The other woman's smile had frozen into place, but her eyes were sharp. "Go? The game hasn't even started yet."

"I'm sorry," she said, hoping a blanket apology would suffice. "My, uh, sister called. She's upset," she stammered. "About today." She stood to the side of the foyer, nodding greetings to Marlee's parents and Ben when she slipped past them. "Don't worry about the pot with the baked beans. Send it with Ben or I'll get it whenever," she told Simon, hoping she sounded far more casual than she felt.

The second Ben cleared the entry, Lori ducked out. "Have a good time tonight," she rambled. She waved when she saw Miss Delia, who was making her way up the walk with a covered plate in hand, and skittered across the lawn to where her car was parked at the curb. When she glanced back, she spotted Simon glaring at her from the center of the knot of people crowding his foyer. Reaching for the door handle, she called back an exuberant "Go, Dawgs!" before making her escape.

Chapter Eight

The day was going to be a total Monday and the sun was barely above the horizon. Lori didn't simply hate sleepless nights; she resented them. She was living a righteous life, and yet she spent hours tossing and turning. For two nights in a row. And losing not one but two nights of sleep fretting over a man who may or may not have a moral compass irked her.

She felt a twinge of guilt for letting the thought creep in. It wasn't true. She might want to vilify him, but Simon did have standards. The problem was, his standards stood in direct opposition to hers.

He had almost kissed her.

After reliving the almost kiss over and over again in her mind for thirty-six straight hours, she wasn't entirely sure if she wanted him to or not.

Dragging her feet, she trudged from the small lot beside the municipal complex to the front of the building. The moment she stepped onto the sidewalk, she was nearly mowed down by a couple jogging past. Stumbling back in her thick-soled utility boots, she let out a startled "Whoa!"

"Sorry!" Marlee Masters called without breaking stride, her golden ponytail gleaming in the early-morning light. Marlee smiled over her shoulder and gave Lori a wave. "Morning, Lori!"

"Morning, Lori," a second, much deeper voice echoed. She blinked and spotted the man who'd caused her sleepless nights striding easily alongside Marlee. Simon Wingate was out jogging like nothing had ever almost happened between them. The jerk.

A tad more incensed than she probably should have been, Lori hustled around the corner and made a bee-line for the main entrance. She barreled into the office with a full head of steam. The second her gaze fell on Ben Kinsella, she blurted, "Are you aware your girl-friend is running around town with Simon Wingate?"

Ben, who'd pulled an overnight shift on their current rotation, looked up and said, "Good morning to you too."

"They're jogging together," Lori said, indignant he wasn't sharing her irritation.

He rolled his neck to stretch it, then launched from his seat and thrust his hands into the air, yawning widely. "Better him than me," Ben said with a tired smile.

"It doesn't bother you?"

Both Ben and Julianne froze for a second, and Lori realized the question had come out with a touch too much vehemence. "Should it?" he asked calmly.

Heat crept up her neck. She stalked to the desk she shared with Mike and dropped her bag into the empty bottom drawer, all too aware she was making a fool of herself over nothing. Her ears burned and she grimaced. "No."

Ben gathered his keys and wallet from his desk drawer. "You must not think much of me if you think I'm going to be intimidated by a guy they used to call Windbag."

Julianne laughed, but Lori's interest was immediately piqued. "Who called him Windbag?"

"Apparently, he was ahead of Marlee at Emory law. She says it took him a couple of months to realize most every kid there had a big-shot parent or two, but he became a cautionary tale. Simon Windbag."

"I see," Lori murmured.

And she did see. All too well. Rather than making her feel superior to Simon and his pompous past, she found herself thrust back to those early days of basic training when every soldier in her company ran their mouths too much.

"Yeah, so let's hope your pal Simon has enough oxygen left in his lungs to keep up, because if there's anyone who won't let him live down a failure to keep up, it's my Marlee."

The pride in Ben's commentary reminded Lori of the way her father used to brag about her shooting skills. An avid outdoorsman, Mateo Cabrera had taught his children everything about firearm safety, precision shooting and the responsibility of hunting only what the family could consume. She'd loved every minute spent under his tutelage. And by the time she was sixteen, she'd won every shooting competition in a three-county radius.

She hadn't been shy about bragging either. When she entered basic training, she drove the other members of her company crazy with her boasting. When she dared to back her words with skill, their drill sergeant had dubbed her Annie Oakley. A nickname she later realized was sort of a backhanded honor. She was labeled a show-off. A fluke. A sideshow sharpshooter.

"Yeah, let's hope he can keep up," she said. "I'd hate to be the one to tell Wendell we broke his grandson."

"Simon will hold up," Ben said gruffly. "Okay, well, I'm out," he announced. "You ladies have a good day. Call if you need me for anything."

Lori waved, then pulled a random file from the drawer and spun back to her desk. When she looked up, she found Julianne's bright green eyes fastened on her. "What?"

"Nothing," the older woman answered, making it clear there was something.

"Out with it," Lori demanded.

Julianne shrugged. "It sounded to me like Ben wasn't the one who was jealous this morning."

"What do you mean?"

"You weren't concerned Marlee was running with Simon. You didn't like that Simon was running with Marlee."

Lori fixed her with a challenging look. "You make no sense."

"It makes perfect sense."

Lori cringed and her cheeks heated. "Why do you think?"

"Because you've never been too terribly interested in Ben and Marlee's relationship up until this point," Julianne replied tartly. "She's not the one you're worried about."

Lori flipped open the file folder she'd pulled from the drawer. "You should take the detective's test, Julianne. You seem to find clues everywhere."

Julianne chuckled. "Say what you want, but I have two eyes. You may think you're inscrutable, but you're not. In fact, you wear your feelings on your face more often than you think."

Insulted, Lori gaped at the woman. "I do not."

Julianne pointed at her. "Outraged," she commented mildly.

"Am not."

"Defensive."

"Okay, stop it." Lori spun away again.

Julianne chuckled. "I'm not nearly caffeinated enough to face this day, and I don't think yogurt is going to cut it this morning. I'm going to run over to see if they have any of those egg-white wraps at the bakery. Do you want anything?"

Lori closed her eyes and envisioned the bakery case at Brewster's. Her mouth watered, but her stomach was twisted in a knot. "Coffee would be great. Something flavored. Caramel macchiato?"

Julianne nodded. "Done." She picked up her purse and strolled to the door. "You'll listen for the phone?"

This was part of the routine. Lori smiled. "And an eye on the door."

Julianne waved. "I'll try not to let Camille hold

me up for too long, but if anything juicy happened over the weekend, I'm going to have to get the details," she warned.

Lori spun back and gave her a salute. "Understood."

The door swung shut behind Julianne, and Lori clicked open the file containing the report she'd taken from Bella Nunes the night Lori had picked her up on Highway 19.

The girl looked so bedraggled and terrified—and young. She seemed so vulnerable—dumped out there without any money or ID. And maybe Lori had jumped in without getting all the facts first—something so unlike her. She was usually the slow, methodical one. But no. Something about Bella Nunes's story lit a fire inside her. She wanted Coulter brought in, and she acted without making sure she had him sewn up. It was the kind of mistake rookies made, and it galled her to know she'd fallen victim to her own emotions.

She was stewing on all of this when the outer door opened. Lori closed the file. "Must not have been any juicy news this morning," she commented, without looking up.

"Exactly what kind of juicy news were you hoping for, Detective Cabrera?" a smooth, deep voice asked in reply.

Lori's head jerked up and she whirled, rising from her chair in one fluid motion. Then she found herself looking directly into the amber eyes of Samuel Coulter.

"What are you—" She caught herself, suddenly

remembering this man was one of the residents of the county she was hired to protect and serve. Plus, she hated to admit he'd managed to burrow under her skin. After all, they hadn't even met. Not officially. "May I help you?" she asked, striving for cool, professional detachment.

He stepped farther into the room, and it was all Lori could do to stand her ground. "I realize we haven't been formally introduced, but I'm guessing I don't need to tell you my name either."

"No. What can I do for you, Mr. Coulter?"

Lori held her breath as he took a long, leisurely look around. Logically, she knew she had no cause to be concerned. She was armed. Skilled in about a dozen different ways to take a man down. Still, she caught herself reaching for the flap on her belt. Ben often teased her about fiddling with it when she felt uneasy or antsy. She curled her hand into a fist and lowered it to her side. The last thing she wanted to do was let Coulter know he had gotten the drop on her.

His quick glance at her hand told her he'd noted the movement. His lips twisted into a tight smile. "I wanted to stop by and speak to you in person."

"Okay," she said, lowering herself into her chair again.

He moved toward her with the loose-limbed grace befitting an invertebrate. Thankfully, Mike had left a bag of clutter he'd cleaned out of his patrol car on the guest chair positioned directly in front of her desk, so she gestured for him to take Julianne's abandoned seat.

He settled himself onto the desk chair, planting the heels of his shoes on the waxed tile floor to keep the chair from rolling. They were expensive-looking leather moccasins. The kind meant to be worn with no socks. Lori hated herself for looking, but she caught a glimpse of tanned ankles sticking out from the hems of his artfully distressed designer jeans.

"What can I do for you, Mr. Coulter?"

"I wanted to come in and tell you directly I had no idea the girl you found working at my refuge was underage or reported missing."

Lori found herself transfixed by the gold flecks in his amber eyes. How could a color so warm appear so...hard?

"Apparently, she's been involved with one of my employees and led him to believe she was older than she is."

He spoke in the soft, honeyed tones of a man born in the Deep South. His diction was cultured. Careful.

"I will, of course, speak to my employee when I am on the premises today—"

She watched him talk. The man was no doubt breathtakingly gorgeous. Lori wondered if he was indeed some kind of demon from hell dallying around with the mere mortals.

"But, since I had to come into town to pick up a package, I wanted to stop in and speak to you in person."

"I appreciate that," she said evenly. "But there was no need. There was an Amber Alert issued, and I was simply doing my job by reporting the sighting. I told your attorney I would have done the same if I spotted her at the Piggly Wiggly."

She focused on a sticky note affixed to Julianne's computer monitor and hoped it appeared she was looking at him. Lori didn't want to appear intimidated, but she really wanted this conversation to be over as quickly as possible.

"Good. Right. As you should." He slapped his hands to his denim-encased thighs and rose gracefully from the wobbly seat.

Coulter paused, a tiny frown line marring the perfection of his high, smooth brow. He peered down at her intently. "Somehow you and I managed to get off on the wrong foot," he said, pairing the sentiment with a smile so tempting she totally identified with old Eve. "I seem to have offended you and I—"

Drawing on the same stubborn streak she'd used to plow through her stint in the army and her mother's disapproval, Lori held up a hand to stop him. In doing so, she also partially obscured his ridiculously attractive face, which helped.

"It's nothing personal, Mr. Coulter."

His smile didn't falter, but it shifted ever so slightly. The wattage had somehow switched from full power to a backup generator. His eyes, though. Those disturbing golden-brown eyes cooled a few degrees. "It feels personal, Deputy."

Such a blunt admission from a man who wielded so much money and power might have thrown her off balance, but she'd handled all manner of manipulation over the years. Coulter was offering up his so-called feelings as bait. But she wasn't biting.

"I'm sorry you feel that way." She tried to keep the smile cordial. "I assure you, in both instances, I was merely following up on information brought to my attention. If either Sheriff Kinsella or Deputy Schaeffer had been the officer Ms. Nunes confided in, they would have done exactly the same thing."

"The sheriff and your fellow deputy didn't feel the need to visit my park," he said, drawling the observation and somehow twisting it into an accusation.

"I wanted to see the place." She didn't offer him any reason why. She didn't believe he deserved one. "I paid the admission."

He lifted a hand, his long, graceful fingers curled slightly, as if he couldn't be bothered to dig down and find the energy to straighten them all the way. He stared directly into her eyes, and though she cringed inside, she didn't look away. "I have security cameras mounted all over the park."

A ripple of foreboding scurried down her spine, but she didn't dare break eye contact, half-afraid he would strike the second she did. "Good to know," she managed to say, her voice surprisingly even. She somehow injected another millimeter into her smile.

His expression was sardonic. "Did you enjoy yourself?"

Lori gripped the edge of her chair, her fingernails digging into the fabric of the cushion. She refused to cede their staring contest. "My sister discovered she didn't have much of a stomach for snakes."

He nodded slowly, but she'd swear the man didn't blink. "Not everyone does. How about you? What did you think?"

Her chin came up a notch. "I'm not afraid of them, but I can't say I'm a fan."

"Fair enough," he said, stretching the words out. He ducked his head, breaking eye contact.

She met him platitude for platitude. "To each his or her own."

He'd made a move for the door when it swung open wide and Julianne appeared with a tray holding to-go cups gripped in one hand, a white pastry bag dangling from her fingers. "You'll never guess who I ran into—" She stopped when she spotted Samuel Coulter standing in front of her desk chair. "Oh, hello."

"Hello." He flashed his powerful smile at poor Julianne, and Lori would swear she saw the woman stagger back a step.

Julianne's gaze shifted from Coulter to Lori, obviously trying to read the mood of the room. Lori wasn't exactly sure what her face showed, but whatever Julianne saw there had the other woman straightening her shoulders and standing her ground. "Am I interrupting or is there something I can help you with?"

"No. Nothing," he assured her with another of those devilish grins. "I was having a quick word with the deputy while I'm in town to pick up a package."

Julianne slid the tray onto her desk and plopped the bag on top. She made a show of glancing at the slim watch on her wrist. "Pick up a package? You're way too early for deliveries." She gazed up at him with wide, innocent eyes, but there was a pinch to Julianne's lips. "The post office doesn't open until ten, and the express delivery trucks don't usually make it to Chet Rinker's store until well after noon."

Coulter's friendly expression faltered. He must have realized Julianne was giving him the bless-your-heart treatment and didn't appreciate it. "Well," he murmured, tucking his hands into his jeans pockets and rocking back on the heels of those spendy leather shoes. "It's a good thing I had my attorney sign for it on Saturday. Thankfully, I won't have to do any sittin' around waiting for the pony express to amble on through."

To her credit, Julianne's smile only dimmed slightly. "Smart thinkin'," she agreed. Sliding past him to reclaim her territory, she busied herself with their coffee and pastries. "Now, I love young Simon, but I don't mind admitting I miss seeing Wendell around town."

"Me too," Lori murmured.

One corner of Coulter's luscious mouth jerked upward, but he stepped away. "Yes, well, if you ladies will excuse me, I'll head on over to see 'young Simon' now." He sauntered to the door. "You have a wonderful day."

Lori caught her bottom lip between her teeth, not daring to even exhale until the door closed behind him.

"My word—" Julianne began, but Lori held up a hand to shush her.

"Wait. The man probably has the hearing of a vampire." She half rose from her chair so she could watch until Coulter had exited the building entirely. Certain he was gone, she dropped back into her seat with a loud whoosh of air. "God, he gives me the heebie-jeebies," she said in a rush.

"Does he?" Julianne eyed her curiously. "I was gonna say he's handsome as Lucifer himself." She rocked back in her chair and fanned herself with her hand.

"I had the exact same thought," Lori admitted.

"Men like him are like catnip to some women," she said, pointing to the windows.

Lori shuddered and shook her head. "Not this woman."

Julianne pried their coffee cups from the carrier. "Not you. But there are plenty of women who would consider trading in the afterlife for some hot times with a dangerous man," she said matter-of-factly. Lori opened her mouth to justify her bias, but Julianne thrust a cup at her.

Lori accepted the cup and sat back with a laugh. "From what I can tell, he is the devil himself."

"Bet you can think about gettin' up to a little naughtiness with Simon Wingate," Julianne teased.

Lori's eyes widened when she took her first sip of the delicious caramel macchiato. "Simon isn't evil."

"Of course he's not. I'm glad you're coming around."

"Coming around on what?" Lori asked, exasperated.

"Rumor has it Simon was mighty happy to see you at his cookout the other night." Julianne gave her a smug smile.

Lori set her cup down on the desk so hard coffee

sloshed out of the tiny opening on the lid. "Whose rumor has what? I was barely there thirty minutes."

"Really? Darn." Julianne's hopeful expression slid from her face. "I told Camille Brewster she had it wrong. It's too bad, though. Simon...he's the whole package."

Lori wasn't prepared to talk about Simon or the kind of package he might be, so she pivoted. "Speaking of packages..." Lori frowned. "What kind of package do you think Coulter had shipped to Simon's office?"

"No idea," Julianne said, extracting her breakfast wrap.

Lori scowled at her coffee cup, feeling put out. The better question was, how come Simon hadn't mentioned anything about this delivery? Of course, what he did for his clients was his business and none of hers. But something had happened between them at his house on Saturday. Maybe that was why the thought of his keeping Coulter's secrets bothered her so darn much.

Chapter Nine

Simon stared at the back of Samuel Coulter's head when the man placed the heavily taped parcel on the Wingate Law Firm's conference table. He slid a hand into his pocket and extracted a small multifunction tool dangling from his key ring. Panic flooded Simon's chest. There was no way he was letting a box marked Perishable and Live Animals be opened in his office. Not by this man.

"Whoa, wait. Are there snakes in there?"

Coulter glanced back at him, his expression amused. "Of course."

"I have no desire to see what is inside."

Coulter fixed his dead-eyed gaze on him. Simon felt about as small as he had the day his professor insinuated his father's involvement in politics made it difficult for Simon to identify with the concept of ethical behavior. "Scared?"

"More like terrified," Simon retorted.

Flipping open the pocketknife, he slit the tape securing the box. "These are hatchlings."

He opened the flaps, then paused to point out the

writing on one of them. It indicated the box contained four nonvenomous ball pythons and gave what Simon assumed was a Latin name for the species. When Dora had seen the labeling, she immediately almost doubled what was already her triple-overtime rate. She also insisted Simon place them in the storeroom, far away from her desk.

There wasn't anything technically illegal regarding the shipment of the snakes, but Simon's gut told him there was something more going on here. Something he couldn't be a part of if he wished to remain within the bounds of legal and social ethics.

"As your attorney, I advise you to wait and open the box when you get home."

"What's the big deal?" Coulter insisted. He lifted a piece of packing material from the top of the box and peered into the cavity. "Normally, I would unbox them immediately upon arrival, but this time I didn't have the timing right." He removed what looked to be a linen bag from the box and began to unwrap the tightly wound drawstring. "These should all be albino morphs," he murmured, opening the bag to reveal a clear plastic container. "I hope they're okay."

Simon swallowed hard, noting the lidded bowl looked disconcertingly similar to the containers in which he'd brought home deli salads for his party. His spine stiffened when he recalled Lori pushing those deli bowls deep into his trash can and making a joke about burying evidence.

Holy hell, he hated this whole thing. Hated his creepy client with his Saturday shipments and sleazy backwoods operation. Hated having to accept delivery of a box that made him so uncomfortable he'd had to document every aspect of his involvement in its custody. Hated having to keep this man's secrets, whether his dealings were aboveboard or not. Hated having to deny himself the pleasure of kissing Lori Cabrera because she'd loathe him if she discovered he'd signed his name on this man's behalf.

"She seems no worse for wear," Coulter said, jolting Simon from his ruminations.

For a minute, he thought Coulter was commenting on Simon's forgoing his natural instincts where Deputy Cabrera was concerned, but the other man slipped the plastic container back into its drawstring bag and wrapped it tight again. To his relief, Coulter returned the tiny snake to her brethren, placed the packing material back on top and loosely secured the flaps.

"I'll check the rest of them when I get home." He hefted the box in his left arm, offering his right to Simon to shake. "I'm sorry to have disrupted your Saturday." He headed toward the office door. "Thanks, Wingate," he called over his shoulder. "Don't forget to bill me for any extra expenses."

Simon held his tongue until he was certain the man was gone. "Yeah, like I'm gonna forget," he muttered.

He strode down the hall to his office. Dora's chair squeaked when she swiveled to glare at him, her animal-print reading glasses perched at the tip of her nose.

"Tell me he didn't open it in here."

"I wish I could," Simon answered dully.

"Wendell Simon Wingate, I told you I didn't want him opening that box on these premises," she scolded.

"The man's billables are what makes it possible for me to pay you quintuple overtime to snap a few pictures."

"Haven't you seen *Snakes on a Plane*?" she asked, incredulous. Dora swiveled away from him. "And… you wouldn't need to pay anyone quintuple overtime if you didn't have men like him for clients."

"This is a vicious circle."

"Don't tell me it's a chicken-and-egg thing. This is a choice," she insisted. "You don't need to sell your soul to make a living here. There are plenty of people who need wills or land transfers done. I spoke to Marlee at the party, and I truly believe she would be happy to let you take some of the Masters family business back. The poor girl is overwhelmed."

"I planned to talk to Marlee myself," he shot back. "I don't need you drumming up business for me."

"Despite all evidence to the contrary." Dora softened. "It was nice of you to tell Marlee to bring her mama and daddy along. I doubt Marlee would have been able to relax otherwise. It's been a tough row to hoe for all of them, what with having to deal with Henry's health issues on top of dealing with the loss of Jeff all over again." She shook her head sadly. "I honestly can't imagine which would be worse— believing your child committed suicide or discovering he'd been murdered."

"Yeah, no idea," Simon agreed. Sighing, he perched his hip on the edge of Dora's desk. "Listen, I'm not a

Coulter fan either, but a part of me thinks it's better this way." When she opened her mouth to argue with him, he held up a hand. "Keep-your-enemies-closer sort of thing. Sometimes, it's better to have the inside scoop on someone you don't trust entirely."

"Yes, but it does no one any good when insider information is protected under attorney-client privilege," she retorted tartly.

Pressing his lips together, he exhaled long and loud from his nose. "You let me worry about what I need to keep quiet."

Dora pushed back from her keyboard and looked him straight in the eye. "I'll tell you the same thing I told Wendell. I have only three years until I can retire with full medical and pull from Dewayne's railroad retirement. I need this firm to stay open and operating until such time. I've given your grandfather almost thirty years of my life. Longer than I had with my husband, God rest his soul."

"Dora—" he assured her.

"I cannot be out looking for a job at my age. I have no desire to relocate."

Simon nodded solemnly, all too aware of all the ways Wendell and Dora were counting on him. "I understand."

"I cannot be your secretary if you get yourself disbarred," she added. "And I cannot buy a place in Kissimmee if I don't have a job."

Placing his hand over his heart, he held her gaze. "Neither Granddad nor I will do anything to mess up your plans."

"You need to find a way to get free of Coulter," she said, nodding to the door.

"Your concerns have been heard and noted." Heaving a sigh, he slid from the desk and made his way to his office. "When you note the billable hours for Saturday, add in about half of your quintuple overtime into the incidental expenses. If I have to pay your extortionist rates, he's gonna split them with me."

Chapter Ten

Lori was surprised to see Ben's door closed when she came in that afternoon. Julianne looked up from the salad she was stabbing with a plastic fork, but her expression was hard to read.

"What's going on?" Lori asked, moving to her desk.

"There's someone from the DEA in there. Ben said they used to work together."

Lori frowned. It was common knowledge that Ben's forced exit from federal duty had left a trail of hard feelings on both sides. Julianne wasn't the only one surprised a DEA agent had ventured all the way to Pine Bluff. Then again, the town had garnered its share of attention from the agency. Lori's stomach rolled when she cast a glance at the closed door.

"How did he act? Do things seem to be going okay in there?"

Three lines appeared on Julianne's forehead. "Well, there's been no yelling," she said cautiously. "Special Agent Simmons is a woman."

"So?" Lori wasn't as surprised by the agent's gender as she was by the accusation embedded in Julianne's statement. "Does that matter?"

Julianne shot another look at the closed door. "I suppose not, but... He said they were coworkers, but he didn't greet her the way he would greet you or me," Julianne said, slanting a pointed look at Lori. "There was hugging and a kiss on the cheek."

Lori fought the impulse to laugh at the condemnation in Julianne's sober assessment. "Dear God, hugging?" she said, playing up her effrontery.

Julianne wadded up a paper napkin and tossed it at Lori. "Don't mock," she snapped.

Lori snagged the napkin from her desk and redeposited it into the trash. "Okay, I won't. I don't think Marlee has anything to worry about. Ben's not about to do anything to jeopardize what he's got going on with her."

Holding her Tupperware container, Julianne swiveled her chair toward Lori. "You don't think he'd ditch the job of backwoods sheriff for another go at being a hotshot federal agent?"

Lori matched Julianne's scowl with one of her own. "You think they're here to lure him back?"

Julianne shrugged. "They've been in there with the door closed ever since she got here."

The door in question opened and both women gave a guilty start. Ben loomed large in the opening. "I thought I heard voices out here. Hey, Lori, would you come in here? I want you to meet Alicia Simmons."

Lori nodded. Shooting a glance in Julianne's direction, she rose from her desk. "Marlee said to tell you she'd call you later this afternoon." She spoke in a voice loud enough to carry well beyond Ben's ears. Behind her, Julianne let out a small hiss of approval.

Ben ducked his head and he stepped aside to let Lori pass into his office. "Uh, okay…"

Lori willed her cheeks not to burn with a telltale flush at the embellishment. "Yeah, sorry. Julianne and I were just—"

Ben closed the door behind them.

A tall, dark-haired woman rose from the chair opposite Ben's desk. She wore gray slacks and a white blouse. Lori figured the pieces would look completely nondescript on any mere mortal, but on this woman they had a certain I-mean-business flair. The woman's smile was cordial but not quite warm. She extended a hand and Lori grasped it.

"You must be Deputy Cabrera," she said in one of those husky Hollywood-siren voices. "I'm Alicia Simmons. Ben and I go way back." She nodded in his direction as he reclaimed his seat behind the desk. "He speaks highly of you," the agent continued as she and Lori sat in the chairs in front of the desk.

Lori inclined her head. "Gratifying to hear. I think highly of him."

Ben cleared his throat. "Okay, lovefest over," he announced, clearly discomfited by their vocal admiration. "Lori, Alicia has some information I think you might find interesting."

Lori fixed a polite gaze on the other woman. "What kind of information?"

"I hear you've been taking a particular interest

in the activities undertaken by a Samuel Coulter," Special Agent Simmons said, pursing her lips. She'd played her trump card.

"What about him?"

Simmons sank back in the chair, practically lounging in the hard wooden seat. She stretched her long legs out and crossed them. "Ben thinks you would be interested to learn we've been watching Coulter for quite some time."

"Watching him for what reason? And for how long is quite some time?" Lori asked, firing off the questions in rapid succession.

Simmons threaded her fingers and let them rest on her flat stomach. "Five years. We picked up on him when he was living in Miami, started to take a closer look when he moved up Jacksonville way. We got even more interested when he moved up here into the middle of nowhere."

"It's not the middle of nowhere," Lori responded, instantly defensive. When she caught Ben's amused glance, she blew out a breath. "Sorry. I hate to break it to you big-city folk, but anywhere outside of Atlanta is not the middle of nowhere."

"My apologies," Special Agent Simmons said with a regal nod. "He moved here to the most rural corner of southern Georgia."

The correction didn't do much to assuage Lori's ire, but the DEA agent went on.

"Coulter isn't exactly a country boy. As I'm sure you know, he was born in Miami and lived there and made an excellent living there. Enough to indulge his…eccentricities," she said, letting her distaste twist her lips. "The Securities and Exchange people took a shot at him, but couldn't make anything stick. But then old Samuel fell in with a new crowd of high-fliers. And I do mean high," she said with a pointed look at Ben.

"You think he was dealing?" the sheriff concluded.

"We think he was…is moving inventory," she corrected. "We were pretty close in South Florida, but he had someone inside who tipped him off. He migrated north to Jacksonville to let things cool off, but he wasn't particularly great at keeping a low profile."

"Probably not one of his strong suits," Lori concurred grudgingly.

"From what we've seen, and what Ben's been telling me, he hasn't exactly managed to blend in here either."

"No, he hasn't." In the blink of an eye, the agent sat up and leaned forward, bracing her elbows on her knees. She gazed at Lori intently. Startled by the sudden movement, Lori pushed back deeper into her own seat. Special Agent Simmons gave the impression of an animal about to pounce.

"Samuel Coulter is a dangerous man. Volatile. Demanding. He surrounds himself mainly with young, impressionable people who are more than willing to do his bidding." She pursed her lips. "Mostly runaways or petty troublemakers. The kind of people few will make a fuss over missing when he's done using them."

"Young people," Lori repeated, horror rippling through her like a shock wave.

Simmons leaned forward in her seat. "Tell me about the girl you found walking along the highway."

It was an order, but the underlying softness in the other woman's request compelled Lori to speak.

"Bella Nunes," Lori said, enunciating the girl's name. Speaking it out loud because, whether they could prove it or not, Lori was convinced she was a victim. "She claimed she was held captive at Coulter's compound. Locked up inside one of the cages with a snake. She was young. A runaway," she said, glancing at Ben as they connected the dots.

Simmons wet her lips and nodded, sliding back in the seat once more. "Would it make you feel better or worse to discover she's not the first young woman to claim such a thing?"

Lori paused to reflect on the question. The truth was, there was no good answer. Nothing was going to make her feel better, and hardly anything could make her feel worse for not being able to do more for the frightened young woman she'd found walking along the side of the highway.

"Neither," she answered at last.

Special Agent Simmons stared at her appraisingly. "Exactly."

Lori's brow furrowed. "Why is the DEA involved? Are you all dabbling in human trafficking these days?"

Simmons chuckled and resumed her slouch, the picture of relaxed repose. "Not exactly," she said in a drawl so soft it sounded dangerous. "We have plenty on our plate with the drugs, but when you add allegations that he's collecting and detaining young women, it becomes even more sinister."

Lori sat straighter. "It certainly does. Do you think he's having them move drugs for him?"

"It's possible. Or they could be another revenue stream for him in addition to whatever product he's funneling through his contacts in South Florida."

Lori stared at her. "Product?"

"Heroin," Simmons supplied.

"Heroin?" Lori shot a look at Ben, then back at the agent beside her. "You think he's moving heroin through Masters County?"

Simmons pursed her lips. "We don't think—we know. The problem is, we're not exactly sure how to catch him doing it."

Ben cleared his throat and Lori swung her attention back to him. "Alicia's going to be moving here for a while. The agency has arranged for her to rent a house. We're setting up a cover that the house belonged to her grandmother and she's inherited it. It will actually be one of the Timber Masters homes," he said with a shrug.

"It's that serious? I mean, for you to move here," Lori asked, unable to mask her surprise.

Alicia Simmons smirked. "I hear all the cool kids are doing it. Ben, Simon Wingate—"

"You know Simon?" Lori interrupted.

"I have heard of Simon," the agent clarified. "We didn't exactly run in the same circles, you understand."

"Right." Lori felt the tension seep from her body. She did understand. Because anywhere other than here in Pine Bluff, she and Simon would not be running in the same circles either.

"I think it would be good if you and Alicia worked together on this." Ben interrupted her line of thinking. "You're both ex-military. Maybe we can say the two of you go back to your time in the service."

Lori glanced over at the other woman. "You were in the army?"

Simmons shrugged. "Navy, but close enough for our purposes."

"True." Lori swung her attention back to Ben. "I don't think you can sell the grandmother story. We don't have many strangers up and move to town, and familial ties run deep in these parts. If you mess with them, someone will uncover the lie whether they mean to or not." She turned the idea over in her mind. "If you're using one of the Timber Masters houses, you'd be better off saying Marlee recruited you to come work for the company."

"Good point," Ben conceded. "I'll talk to Marlee. I'm sure she'd be on board."

For her part, Alicia Simmons simply held up her hand to indicate she was open to anything. "Whatever you think is best. This is your town."

Lori looked from one to the other. They were serious. And they were right. This was her town, even if she never fit in. She wasn't the insecure young girl she'd once been. In truth, she wasn't sure she wanted to fit in. Either way, of the three of them sitting in this room, she was the one who was the expert on Pine Bluff and the rest of Masters County.

She wasn't being conceited when she realized they were right to leave it up to her to lead the charge on this. Small towns were insular, and whether she thought the town's residents looked at her and her family as being different due to their ethnicity, they were locals. She was going to be able to get better answers from them than any stranger would. Particularly strangers who carried badges and credentials issued by anyone whose authority they did not inherently respect.

The DEA's sweeps of the area, while justified, left a mess in their wake. A mess the residents of Masters County had to clean up. Not everyone had a particularly favorable view of the federal agency regardless of their stance on drug trafficking in the area. Most of the county's citizens understood and appreciated the need to shut those operations down, but they did not appreciate the economic hardships and familial destruction that followed.

"Yes, I think it would be best to use Timber Masters for cover. Almost everybody in the county has a connection to the company either directly or indirectly. You wouldn't necessarily be undercover…more like hidden in plain sight."

Lori tugged at her lower lip as she mulled over possible complications. She saw no downside. Though her own personal agenda may have had more to do with apprehending any of the men involved in possibly abusing young girls, she wasn't at all sad to help disrupt any supply line of illegal narcotics from flowing into the country.

"How are you thinking you'll be able to breach his security to catch him with the heroin?" she asked Special Agent Simmons.

The other woman sat up in her chair, her posture alert and engaged. "We're not entirely sure yet, but we are sure it's coming through him." She paused and cast a glance at Ben. At his nod of encouragement, she spoke more freely. "I think it has something to do with the snakes."

"The snakes?"

Lori shook her head. She didn't want to appear dim, but she couldn't see how snakes could have anything to do with the transportation of the world's most dangerous opiate.

"Heroin is smuggled in more ways than you can imagine," Alicia said gravely. "We find people smuggling in every body cavity you can imagine, and not only humans." She pulled a face. "The snake trade is one we've been eyeballing for a while. It consists of mainly private breeders and suppliers. They do much of their business online or through mail order. So, yeah, it wouldn't be unheard of for someone to ship a snake stuffed with packets of narcotics. They used them in cocaine trafficking back in the day."

Lori gaped at the other woman in disbelief. Her brain had gotten hung up somewhere around the time body cavities were mentioned, and stalled out entirely when the possibility of smuggling drugs inside of live snakes was mentioned. She was about to say something about how outlandish it all sounded when she remembered the mysterious package Coulter had had delivered to Simon Wingate's office.

Her heart gave a dull thump. Simon Wingate couldn't possibly be involved in this situation, she assured herself. Simon Wingate had plans for a political career. He wouldn't jeopardize his future for anyone, client or no.

At least, she didn't think he would.

The truth was, Simon could be in on the whole thing. Could this be how a future politician planned to finance his campaign? Samuel Coulter and everyone and everything associated with him seemed too seedy for Simon Wingate. Or so she consoled herself.

The package delivery bothered her, though.

Lori ducked her head, racking her brain for every single memory of Saturday night's cookout. Had he mentioned receiving a box on his client's behalf? No, she was fairly sure he hadn't. If it had been something simple and innocent like accepting the delivery while his client was out of town, wouldn't he have said so? Wouldn't he have complained about having to go into the office on a Saturday to receive this mysterious package? She would have, if she were Simon.

"What are you thinking?"

Ben's question jarred her from the depths of her thoughts. "I was wondering how it all works," she said with a wary half smile. Ben narrowed his eyes, but Special Agent Simmons was more than happy to jump in.

"It's pretty common. Most carriers, including the US Postal Service and United Parcel Service, have stopped allowing live animals to be shipped, but there are private couriers and other express services willing to handle the packages. Federal law requires live animals are labeled with the common as well as scientific names for the contents, but it's all legal." She pursed her lips. "You can ship anything from a long baby boa to a full-grown snake. Oh, and they can only ship nonvenomous species."

"Nonvenomous," Lori repeated in a daze.

"Of course, they ship the venomous ones too, though." The special agent gave a wan smile.

"I can't believe there's no oversight," Lori said, aghast.

"There is, but if you were inspecting or getting paid an hourly rate, would you open every box of snakes?" She sank into her chair again and let out a heavy sigh. "I can't blame them. The problem is, they start to believe those are sources deemed reliable based on past inspections. But we know they are the most dangerous kind of all."

SINCE THEY WERE agreed Lori would be point person with the locals, the next morning she made Rinker's Pharmacy her first stop. Chet Rinker's place had long served as the town's express package pickup and drop-off point. If Samuel Coulter had shipped any parcel containing live animals, it would have gone through Mr. Rinker's store. Lori wasn't sure how these things worked, but it was possible the man had a record of deliveries made in the area.

She hung back, sipping a cup of coffee from the

bakery and waiting for the line in front of the cash register to dwindle. Marjorie Rinker, Chet's wife, was working the line while he bustled around behind her filling orders without making eye contact with the people at the counter.

Lori waited patiently, enjoying her coffee and letting her speculation run wild. She was so lost in thought she jumped when the bell above the door jingled behind her. She did a double take when she realized the woman bustling into the store was her own—"Mama?"

Sophia Castillo-Cabrera whirled, her expression a mixture of surprise and mortification. "*Mija?* What are you doing here?"

Lori nodded toward the counter. "I need to ask Mr. Rinker some questions, but I was waiting for the line to die down. What are you doing here?"

"Me?" With her hand pressed to her chest and her eyes wide, Lori's mother was the picture of innocence. Unfortunately, she'd oversold it with her delivery. "I'm here to pick up odds and ends."

Lori frowned at her mother. Sophia was many things, but a good liar was not on the list. "Mama, is everything okay?"

Her mother's mouth pinched into a tight line and her dark eyes narrowed to slits. When she was younger, Lori would have quavered at what she termed her mother's angry face. Now, studying her up close, she could honestly say her expression was more agitated than aggravated.

"The doctor gave me a prescription to help with some…personal issues," she said at last.

Lori swallowed a scoff. Her mother didn't appear to be in the mood for jokes. "What kind of medication?"

"I'm starting to have hormonal changes, not that it's any of your business. The doctor called in a prescription for me, but I'm fine." With a flick of her wrist, her mother dismissed any possible discussion of what Lori could only assume was the onset of menopause. "What do you need to talk to Mr. Chet about?" She moved closer and pitched her voice low. "Are you in trouble?"

The conversation shifted from menopause to pregnancy so fast Lori felt the whiplash. "No, Mama. I have to talk to him about police business."

"Ah." Her mother's hand flew to her chest again, but this time she gave herself a comforting pat. "Okay. Okay, good."

Lori shook her head. "I can't believe you thought— It would be an actual miracle, Mama," she said gravely. "I'm sorry to disappoint you."

Sophia sniffed, clearly miffed. "I'm not disappointed." Her expression softened. "I'm never disappointed in you, *mija*. I just miss you sometimes."

"I miss you too, Mama."

Lori was tempted to confide in her mother, tell her that sometimes she wished her life were exciting enough to make that kind of trouble a possibility. She wanted to tell her about Simon Wingate and the almost kiss. Confess that sometimes she mourned the loss of Jeff Masters and what they might have had. Mostly, she wanted to talk to her mother in the openhearted way they had spoken with one another in the years before the military tore her down and rebuilt her.

The bell above the door rang again.

They spun in unison, and Lori saw Julianne panting in the open doorway, her eyes darting from Lori to her mother and back. She looked scared and remained uncharacteristically silent.

"Is everything okay?" Lori asked, taking a step closer to the door.

"I, uh…" Her gaze slid toward Lori's mother. "I need to speak to you. Official business."

Sophia took the hint. "Don't mind me." She gave Lori's arm a reassuring pat and moved past her. "I'll go get in line. We'll talk later."

When her mother was gone, Lori gave her full attention to Julianne. Lowering her voice, she asked, "What's wrong?"

"Lena is in the office," she whispered, nervously glancing at Sophia's back.

"What?" Reflexively, Lori raised her wrist to glance at her watch. "She should be in school."

Julianne swallowed hard. "She cut. Obviously." Then, taking Lori's elbow, she drew her out the door. "You need to come. She's upset."

Lori's heart began to pound and she quickened her step. "Upset about what? Did she say?"

Julianne huffed and puffed, trying to keep pace. "She only wanted to talk to you, but since I was the only one in the office at the time, I was able to get her to calm down and talk to me. I guess some friend of hers wasn't at school and she called the girl's house and her parents thought she was with Lena—"

"Jasmine!" Lori broke into a run.

She burst into the office and found her sister sitting at Julianne's desk, a can of soda clasped between her hands. Ben stood near Lori's desk, close enough to keep tabs on the teenager, but not so close as to loom over her. He was holding her sister's glitter-cased phone in his big hands.

"What is it? What's happening?" Lori demanded, dropping down to look her sister in the eyes. "Is it Jas?"

Lena nodded mutely, her fingertips pressing into the aluminum can as tears spilled over the edge of her lashes.

Lori glanced up at Julianne before pressing on with her questions. "She wasn't at school today?"

"No. And when I called her cell, it kept going to voice mail, so I called her mom to see if she was sick or something," Lena said, her voice creaky from crying. "She said she was supposed to be at our house."

Lori nodded to show she was following. "But she hasn't been to our house," she prompted, oddly heartened that her sister still considered her a member of the household, whether she lived there or not.

"No. And when I looked at her PicturSpam account, all I saw were pictures of that guy," Lena said, anger and frustration starting to overtake her fear.

Lori cast a quick look in Ben's direction before pushing for more. "The guy from Reptile Rendezvous?"

"Yeah. Rick," Lena confirmed.

"Rick Dale, according to his profile," Ben added.

Lori's head jerked up. When she'd spoken to Jasmine's mother about what Lena had told her, Keely insisted that they kept a close eye on their daughter's accounts and hadn't seen anything about any guy in particular in her feed. "Is he on there? On Jasmine's page?"

Ben nodded. "All over it."

She stretched a hand toward Ben, gesturing for the phone. "I talked to her mom. Keely Jones said they hadn't seen anything about a guy on her pages."

"You talked to her mom?" Lena demanded, redirecting some of her anger Lori's way. "When? What did you say?"

He shot a look at Lena, then held the phone out to Lori. Unperturbed by Lena's adolescent outrage, she took it and began to scroll. "I talked to her that day. She needed to know what was up. Jas has no business hanging around guys that much older than her." She swiped back to the top of the feed, then frowned as she noted the username showing there. "Le-Le? Does Jas have more than one PicturSpam account?"

She looked up just in time to see the lightning bolt of guilt cross her sister's face. Thankfully, the Cabrera stubborn streak kicked in. Lena jutted her jaw, then shrugged. "I don't know. Maybe."

Heaving a sigh, Lori shoved to her feet. Meeting

Ben's gaze, she translated. "That's teenager for 'Yeah. Duh.' In case you don't speak the language."

Turning to Julianne, she said, "Call Keely. She has to be beside herself with worry. We can solve the mystery of the multiple accounts and start piecing together info for an Amber Alert."

Focusing on Ben again, she tipped her chin up exactly as her sister had a moment before. "I'm going across the hall to see about getting a warrant to search Coulter's property. You coming?"

Chapter Eleven

"You cannot issue a warrant to search my client's property based on a hunch," Simon Wingate stated flatly. He couldn't believe he'd actually managed to get the words out. His tongue felt thick. His head buzzed with questions he wasn't entirely sure he wanted answered.

The Amber Alert had come across his phone while he was pouring his second cup of coffee. The first cup he'd downed transformed into a burbling sludge in his gut. He scanned the alert. The scant few facts he saw made his knees go weak.

Jasmine Jones. Sixteen. Last seen in a silver Toyota Corolla. Florida plates.

Jasmine. Lori Cabrera's little sister had a best friend named Jasmine. He'd barely absorbed the information when Dora popped her head into the office kitchenette to inform him he was needed in Judge Nichols's chambers concerning a search warrant. He didn't have to ask what the summons was about or who was likely leading the charge to have his client's property turned upside down and shaken until young Jasmine fell out.

Now here he was, standing opposite Harrison Hayes, Ben Kinsella and Lori Cabrera, and hating the position he was in. Hated opposing people he wanted to call friends. He was duty bound to argue against the issuance of a search warrant for Samuel Coulter's property. It didn't matter if he personally thought the request was reasonable. His opinion didn't count.

Neither did the "evidence" Lori's sister had produced. In the end, they had some screenshots of a social media profile of a young man named Rick Dale, who claimed he worked at the Reptile Rendezvous, and Marialena Cabrera's word that the missing girl, Jasmine Jones, was likely with this Dale character.

While he understood the fire fueling Lori's insistence on obtaining a search warrant, Simon could tell Hayes was aware they didn't have a leg to stand on. His job, his only job, was to make sure nobody trampled on his client's right to privacy. Part of him shuddered to think too hard about what they might find if they had free access to Coulter's property.

"Your Honor, they don't have a shred of evidence connecting my client directly to the disappearance of this young woman—"

"She's not a woman. She's sixteen," Lori interjected.

"Deputy, please," Judge Nichols admonished mildly. "You're only here as a courtesy. Don't make me ask you to leave."

Simon picked up where he'd been cut off. "While I understand time is of the essence, and admittedly there may be some connection between my client and the young man Jasmine Jones was allegedly seeing socially, there's no just cause for my client's premises to be searched."

"Your Honor, the courts generally grant the authorities some leeway when the safety of a minor is involved," Hayes argued.

"We have no evidence anyone was abducted, and absolutely nothing connecting her disappearance directly to my client." Simon chanced a glance at Ben, not daring to look directly at Lori. "There are no legal grounds to search Mr. Coulter's property."

"Your Honor, last week we had another young woman claim—" Lori began.

Judge Nichols held up his hand to stop her. "While I appreciate your dedication, Deputy, Mr. Coulter was not charged in that instance, so I cannot allow it to have any bearing here," he reminded her.

Simon homed in on Lori, imploring her to see reason. "A search warrant grants you too much opportunity to infringe on my client's right to privacy on his own property." He raised both hands to indicate his own frustration, then tried to reframe the sheriff's department's request into something more reasonable. "Can you set up surveillance? You can watch for them from the highway. I don't believe Mr. Coulter's employees live on-site. You might catch Rick Dale coming or going."

"I don't have unlimited resources, Simon," Ben Kinsella said dryly. "We're not exactly staffed for stakeouts."

"Listen, I want Jasmine safe with her family too,

but I feel compelled to state for the record even seeking a search warrant for my client's property could be seen as a gross overreach. My client is already feeling put on the spot. I'd hate for him to feel he needs to go on the offensive."

He locked eyes with Hayes. "Which is why I appreciate you calling me in here for this—" he shifted his gaze to the judge "—informal discussion about a missing girl's possible whereabouts."

Heaving a heavy sigh, Judge Nichols ran a gnarled hand over his face, pulling at his jowls. When he opened his eyes, he looked directly at Simon. "November can't come soon enough for me," he said flatly. "Whoever wins the seat is more than welcome to it."

Simon inclined his head. "I understand, Your Honor."

The judge shook his head. "No, I don't think you *do* understand. This kind of stuff might be commonplace up in the city, but these past few years here—" He broke off, shaking his head in disbelief. "I can't for the life of me imagine why your grandfather wants this job."

"Your Honor…" Lori began again.

The judge only shook his head. "Unfortunately, Deputy Cabrera, Mr. Wingate is correct. I need evidence Mr. Coulter had something to do with this young lady's disappearance." Sliding his gaze to Hayes, he added, "Bring me one shred of evidence connecting him to her, and we'll continue this 'informal conversation' about search warrants."

When they shuffled from the judge's chambers, the sheriff was careful to place himself between Simon and Lori, but there was no hiding the deputy's chagrin.

"Well, that went about as expected," Hayes said when they entered the larger office space that housed the district attorney's offices.

"I can't believe you took such weak evidence to him," Simon said, shaking his head.

Hayes shrugged. "I came up against an immovable object."

Steps ahead of them, Lori led the charge. She didn't look back. She didn't speak to anyone. She just made a beeline for the door leading to the municipal building's atrium, no doubt anxious to get back on her own turf.

"Lori, wait," he called after her.

She didn't break stride. Instead, she raised one hand in a rude gesture and kept walking forward, her other palm extended to push open the door.

"Give her some time," Ben advised. "This is hitting close to home for her."

"I understand," Simon snapped. "I'm not the enemy here."

Both the sheriff and the district attorney looked at him, their expressions curious. "No," Ben began slowly. "She only sees you defending her enemy, which puts you squarely on the wrong team."

"Ben, I'm not—"

"I know," Ben said succinctly. "It's not an easy pill to swallow. Not for any of us."

Simon stood rooted to the spot as Ben disappeared into the offices across the hall. Through the glass walls, he saw him stop and speak to Lori, who was clearly agitated. He wanted to go over there and try to reason with her, but there wasn't any point. He might have the law on his side, but working within the law didn't necessarily mean he was right.

"She'll cool off." Hayes spoke quietly.

When Simon glanced over his shoulder, he saw the district attorney staring across the fishbowl atrium into the law's side of the Masters County law and justice center.

"I hope so," Simon murmured. Facing the other man, he asked, "Why'd you even take it in there? There was no way Nichols was going to approve a warrant."

Hayes nodded. "She came storming in here while Judge Nichols was hitting the coffeepot." He shrugged. "He heard her and the judge thought he might save a lot of running around if we got everyone in the room and hashed it out."

Simon nodded, and his gaze strayed back to the woman across the hall. Even through multiple panes of glass, he could see the anger shimmering off her like heat rising from a sunbaked road. "I should never have mentioned a stakeout. She'll park her car right outside those gates every day and every night," he grumbled.

"Yes, she probably will." Hayes peered at him. "You have three options."

Simon jerked, startled by the man's blunt assessment. He tore his attention from Lori. "Oh, yeah? What are those?"

"One, you walk away knowing you did everything legally necessary to save your client a hassle, to heck with a sixteen-year-old girl—"

"I'm not a monster, Harry," he growled.

"Okay, so option two would be to maybe put the bug in your client's ear about how this girl's disappearance is, uh, reflecting on him, and see if he is willing to voluntarily allow the sheriff's department to ease their minds about her being at his place."

"Yeah, I don't think he's feeling overly friendly to the people on our side of the building these days."

"With good reason." Hayes nodded to the sheriff's offices. "One of Ben's friends from the DEA came to call yesterday."

"Are you insinuating they might be coming here to investigate my client for some reason?"

"I'm saying it seems your client has a reputation."

Simon's gaze narrowed. "I'm representing him, not dating him."

"No, your tastes run more to curvy brunettes," Hayes answered, darting a meaningful glance at the windows.

"You don't know what you're talking about."

"You do, but for the life of me, I can't see how you'll ever get over the Coulter-shaped hurdle."

Tiring of Hayes's lecturing, he spun to face the other man head-on. "You said three things."

"Help her," Hayes answered with a shrug.

"Help her how? I have an obligation to my client."

"Help her by helping your client avoid another entanglement with the law," the other man said patiently. "She's not worried the girl has taken off with Coulter. She's worried she's with one of the guys who works for him. Coulter's employees are not your clients. I'd lay odds if your client gets wind the sheriff suspects there's another underage girl hiding out in his refuge, he'll turn the place upside down to get her out of there." He paused, and they both glanced to where Lori sat hunched over her desk, her phone pressed to her ear. "Try helping her in other ways."

Simon let his head fall forward and rubbed the back of his neck. "Okay," he said quietly, his mind racing through all the ways he could broach the topic with Coulter. "Okay. I'll see what I can find out about this Rick guy." He gave his head a shake, his expression grim. "I'm pretty sure I saw him at the Daisy the other day."

"Oh?" Hayes look intrigued.

"I can't say for sure. Mostly I remember the car." He grimaced. "You know how kids take a perfectly good subcompact and trick it out with the popping exhaust and the big wings on the back? It was one of those."

The other man fixed him with a pointed look. The kind that said Simon was missing something by a mile. "Maybe you should share your information with Deputy Cabrera."

Simon rolled his eyes at the man's deliberate enunciation. "Maybe, but I'm not sure she wants to hear anything I have to say."

"The only thing we're certain of right now is a sixteen-year-old girl has not been seen by her parents since Sunday morning." He paused to let the assertion sink in. "We've lost almost forty-eight hours and the clock is ticking."

Swallowing the hard lump of truth, Simon headed for the door himself. "Right." When he was halfway out into the atrium, he remembered his manners. "Thanks, Harry. I'll talk to you later."

Simon didn't look back to see if Hayes was watching when he crossed the lobby; he didn't need to. He could feel the man's gaze trained on the back of his head. Hayes was right. Rick Dale was not his client. Coulter was. Simon was free to share what little information he had on the guy without violating his client's privilege.

When he stepped through the door to the sheriff's department, the occupants fell quiet. Ben even glowered at him, his arms crossed over his chest.

"Can we help you, Simon?" the sheriff asked, cool and controlled. His calm helped counter some of the heat in Lori's dark eyes.

"Yeah, I, uh…" Simon leaned to the side, hoping to make eye contact with the fuming woman behind her gatekeeper. "I wanted to tell you I think I've seen this Dale guy around town."

"Great," she said sarcastically. "Thanks for the intel."

"Actually, it *is* great," Ben interrupted. "If Simon remembers him, maybe other people will too. We can start canvassing."

"I'm also pretty sure I've seen his car." Reaching into his pocket, Simon extracted his cell and swiped at the screen until the information contained in the Amber Alert came up again. He frowned at the information and searched his memory. "It was a Toyota. Older model. I don't remember looking at the plates."

"Thanks for confirming what we already know," Lori said drolly. "We'll contact your office if we need you to be even more unhelpful than you already are."

Tired of being the target of her ire, Simon switched his attention to Ben. "You don't think it would be helpful to note that the car was more primer gray than silver? Or about the oversize airfoil wing?"

Ben dug into his shirt pocket and extracted a small notebook with a golf pencil jammed through the binding rings. "Airfoil wing? A spoiler?"

"For the sake of simplicity, yes. They're technically different, but you get what I mean."

Ben frowned. "What's the difference?"

"A spoiler creates better airflow and decreases drag, but a wing deflects airflow to add drag."

"Why would you add drag?" Ben asked, his pencil poised.

"Well, on actual race cars, to improve stability and cornering at high speed. These guys probably just think it looks cool."

"Could you two make a date to play *Grand Theft Auto* some other time?" Lori asked, agitation pitching her voice higher than usual. "It's got a wing thing on the back. Anything else you care to share, Counselor?"

Simon resisted the urge to roll his eyes. "The usual

aftermarket tricks, taillight covers and I'd guess xenon headlights. The exhaust was modified."

"Roar or popper?" Ben asked.

"More of a popper, but they had a whistle effect in there, I think."

Lori rose from the desk, dividing an incredulous look between Ben and himself. "How is the sound of his muffler supposed to help us find Jasmine?"

"Because people notice noisy cars," Ben murmured, jotting a few more notes. "Anything else?"

Simon shook his head. "If I think of anything more, I'll be in touch."

Nodding, Ben pivoted on his heel and headed for his own desk. "I'll send the information to the state coordinator and they can distribute it to surrounding areas. Thanks, Simon."

"Yeah, anything I can do." His response had been automatic, but he regretted the words. Not because he didn't mean them, but because they sounded trite.

"Yes, thank you so much, Simon," Lori said with a sneer. "You threw us a Froot Loop when we need a life preserver, but hey, you're still a great guy."

"Hey, now," Ben chided from his office.

"Lori," Julianne gasped at the same time.

Lori stared at him, practically daring him to protest her treatment of him. He wouldn't give her the satisfaction. He would do everything he could do—legally and ethically—to help find the missing girl, but he wasn't going to open his client up to an abuse of power because he wanted to make nice with the pretty deputy with the giant chip on her shoulder.

At last, Lori plucked a business card from the holder on the desk and handed it to him. "Please feel free to pass along any other information you would like to share, Counselor."

He took the card and nodded to Julianne as he passed her desk. "I'll call if I come across anything useful."

He hit the push bar on the glass door hard and had one foot in the atrium before he heard Julianne call after him, "Thank you, Simon."

Looking back through the glass, he saw Julianne's hand lowering slowly to her side, her expression anxious and guilt stricken. Lori stood with her arms crossed over her chest and her gaze locked on him. He shouldn't care. What did it matter to him if a Hicksville sheriff's deputy looked at him like he was something she'd scraped off her shoe?

He did care.

Because he did, Simon shoved his way out of the Masters County Municipal Center, hell-bent on proving himself innocent, though presumed guilty by association.

Back in his office, Simon closed the door and dialed his father's number. It went immediately to voice mail. Sighing because he was all too aware he was letting himself in for a lecture on legal ethics, he swiped the screen again and hit the speed dial for his grandfather. Wendell answered on the second ring.

"Have you burned my office down?" he asked in lieu of a hello.

"Not yet," Simon replied. "The day is young."

"Two phone calls in one week," Wendell commented. "Why do I get the feeling you're not calling simply because you enjoy talking to your dear old granddad?"

"I do enjoy talking to you," Simon retorted.

"We've never talked this much," Wendell challenged. "I'm not complaining, mind you."

"Sounds like complaining."

"If I were to complain about anything, it would be the godforsaken rubber-chicken lunch I have coming up. Why don't you tell me what it is you need?" his grandfather suggested.

"Absolution?"

The whoosh of a heavy exhalation rushed through the line. "Hoo-boy. What have you done?"

"Nothing yet."

"What are you thinking about doing?" his grandfather pressed.

"Firing Samuel Coulter," Simon answered honestly.

There was a prolonged silence on the other end. Finally, his grandfather asked, "Okay. Why?"

"Why?" Simon gave a short laugh. "Because the guy's creepy?" he said, only half joking.

"Creepiness isn't reason enough. You took the man's retainer. You need a genuine conflict or cause in order to sever the relationship."

"I don't think I'm capable of giving the man an unbiased defense."

"If he's willing to accept your reason, good for you. I have to warn you, you're never going to make it through a life in law or politics without having to deal with some real scumbags," Wendell said bluntly. "If you can't get over feeling squeamish from time to time, you'd better start thinking about an alternative career plan."

"To be honest, I'm starting to think so too," Simon said quietly.

"Are you considering giving up the law entirely?" his grandfather asked, a note of worry in his question.

"No," Simon answered without a thought. "I'm not into handling the criminal stuff—I can tell you that. I don't mind doing the wills and probate, real-estate transactions, normal kind of stuff."

"Son, if we could all choose to deal only with the tidier aspects of the law, we would, but in a small-town practice, you take what comes to you."

"Even if the people coming to you are flat-out wrong?"

"Do you know for a fact your client is actively engaged in breaking the law or making you a party to his alleged illegal activities?"

"No." Simon couldn't keep the sulky note out of his admission. "I know there's something wrong about this guy and I don't want anything to do with him."

"Your opinion wouldn't be influenced by Deputy Lori Cabrera, would it?"

"Lori?" Simon tried to sound amused but was pretty sure he came off defensive.

"I hear the two of you were chatting it up at your cookout the other night," Wendell commented mildly.

Simon snorted but sat up straighter in his seat. "Your informants passed along faulty information."

"Were you, or were you not, seen speaking with Ms. Cabrera in an intimate manner?" his grandfather asked, his careful but unwavering delivery making it abundantly clear how he'd managed to win over so many juries. It made Simon wonder if he could go after a witness with the same steady and undaunted determination.

Instead, he did a fair rendition of the politician shuffle step. "I had a conversation with Ms. Cabrera Saturday evening. We ate some chips and salsa," he said snidely. "Hardly what I would call intimate."

"Mmm. Miss Sophia's salsa, I imagine," he murmured. Then, clearing his throat, he pressed on. "Simon, I understand you and Lori are on opposite sides when it comes to dealing with Coulter's issues, but I would caution you to think long and hard about making an enemy of this man. I understand you may feel a—" he paused, searching for the right word "—fondness for Lori. She's an easy young woman to like. Last I heard, you had no intention of making Pine Bluff your home on a permanent basis, and because *I'm* fond of her, I would hate to hear of Miss Lori being misled or ill-treated in any way."

Simon hissed his frustration through clenched teeth, but his grandfather continued.

"I thought you had aspirations of the political nature," he reminded Simon. "People who have such aspirations need to think twice about alienating the multimillionaire in their backyard."

Simon propped his elbow on the arm of the chair and ran his index finger over his top lip, allowing his grandfather's warning to sink in. "I'm aware of all this."

"And you want to fire him?" Wendell prompted. "Clients with his bank balance and messy legal needs are not going to come along every day. A defense attorney makes a good living off a man who can't seem to keep himself out of trouble."

"Maybe I'm not meant to be a defense attorney," Simon admitted.

"You've certainly mastered the art of the circular argument," Wendell said dryly. "The best I can tell you is to talk to the man. Be frank and honest with him. Get a good feeling for how he might respond."

"Right," Simon said, nodding. "I will."

"And if you *are* interested in Lori Cabrera, I suggest you do the same with her," he added. "She's a bright young woman. Strong-minded too. She responds well to people who are direct with her. If you're looking for a distraction while you're there in town, I suggest you look elsewhere."

"Granddad—"

"The woman's a sharpshooter, Simon. I care about her, but in the end, I'm more concerned with keeping you alive. Not only can she pick you off, but she's clever enough to stage it like an accident."

Simon laughed. "Thanks. I've already been warned."

"No doubt by the woman herself," Wendell added with a chuckle.

Chapter Twelve

Lori sat slumped in her patrol car silently fuming.

A stakeout.

She gave her head a slow shake and repositioned her left arm on the sill of the open driver's-side window. The radar gun she held was sadly outdated, but the latest and greatest the county had to offer. She figured it was worth the taxpayers' time and money to sit out on Highway 19 for a while, watching to see if she could pick off any speeders heading toward Pine Bluff. If she happened to see a silver or gray Toyota Corolla with or without one of those ridiculous wing things stuck to the back, well, good.

True to his word, Ben had relayed the additional information Simon had given them to the coordinator so the other law enforcement agencies in the area had it too. A few of the details had been held back from what was being released to the general public, a precaution frequently used to be sure they were dealing with the possible perpetrator rather than one of the many "hot tips" they gathered by the bushel.

She sank down deeper into her seat. The conversation she'd had with Lena had left her feeling frayed at the edges, but speaking recently to Mr. and Mrs. Jones about their missing daughter shredded her heart.

When she had originally spoken with Keely, Lori discovered Jasmine's parents had no idea she'd even been speaking to any boy, much less an older one. A stranger. Say what you would about small towns, but there was a comfort in knowing all the kids who went to school with your kid. Most of the time, you also knew their parents, where they lived and what teams they played on. The thought of their daughter running off with a guy who was a complete unknown was incomprehensible to them.

Lori could understand their bewilderment. She had known Jasmine since she and Lena had met in kindergarten and become fast friends. The girl wasn't some impulsive rebel. She wasn't a hardheaded teenager who defied her parents' every wish. She was a sensible girl. Jas was exactly the kind of girl most parents wouldn't worry about, which made this all so much more troubling.

A sleek black sports car stuck its nose out from one of the farm access roads. She narrowed her eyes when the driver turned onto the highway heading for town. Lori slumped low and instinctively reached for the radar gun. Sports cars were not the preferred mode of transportation in this neck of the woods. Pickup trucks were more practical. Heck, her own mother drove an SUV. Only one man in this area drove a Dodge Viper. Coulter.

She clocked him at a sedate three miles per hour over the posted limit. He was keeping his speed under tight rein for her benefit. The man had the cojones to lift a hand and wave at his rearview mirror.

"Of all the times to become a law-abiding citizen," she grumbled, watching the car slink by at a modest pace.

She did her best to ignore the man and his ridiculous car. The rip of a powerful motor split the air. He'd gunned it the second he was out of range. Lori scowled in his direction. Even if she flipped on her lights and floored the accelerator, there was no way she could catch up to a car built for speed. Though she loathed the man, Coulter was not her prey on this day.

The man wasn't above the law, was he?

She picked up the radio microphone and toggled the key. "Base, do you read me?"

Julianne's voice came across. "Ten-four, number three. Go ahead."

"If Ben has a mind to hop into his car, a certain gentleman in a Dodge Viper is heading to town at an unsafe speed."

Julianne chuckled. "You didn't try to give pursuit?"

"He didn't punch it until I was well out of range."

Julianne came back on the channel. "Chief says to tell you he's saddling up."

Lori pressed the button on the side of the mic again. "Ten-four. Happy hunting."

Feeling better, she stretched her neck and let her head roll from side to side. She'd let Ben and Alicia from the DEA deal with Coulter. For now. All she wanted was to get Jasmine home safe and sound.

She watched and waited. If people who wrote the scripts for television cop shows were only keyed in to how much of her day was spent simply watching and waiting, they'd opt for a life of crime simply to break up the monotony. The back of her uniform shirt stuck to her skin. A fine film of perspiration formed on her upper lip. Then the radio crackled to life, rattling her out of her rumination.

Lori smiled when Ben's deep voice came through the speaker. "The county coffers should be about three to five hundred dollars richer soon," he said, his voice hearty with pride.

Lori chuckled but didn't pick up the mic to respond. There was no need. They'd been reduced to harassment rather than action, and the knowledge irked. Gnats. That was all they were to men like Coulter. Pesky and annoying. If the county could occasionally profit off the man's hubris, who was she to pass it up?

"Heading back to the ranch," Ben said gruffly. "Thanks for the heads-up."

Lori grabbed the mic and keyed it. "Ten-four. Believe me when I tell you it was my pleasure."

"Oh, I believe you," Ben returned. "Over."

Lori placed the mic back on the hook and started the engine. Sitting here was only making her feel more helpless than ever. She'd visit Simon, see if she could coax some information out of him about his client. After all, a girl's life depended on it.

SIMON WAS SETTLED in at one of the rickety picnic tables the Daisy Drive-In had to offer, wishing he was anywhere else. The couple who'd been eating there jumped up and scurried away when Coulter fixed his dead-eyed stare on them. So here he was.

"I bet you're used to fancier business lunches than this," Coulter said, unwrapping a greasy cheeseburger loaded with everything.

Simon sat carefully, hoping to avoid picking up a splinter anywhere delicate. "This seems to be where I take most of my lunches these days."

Coulter took a huge bite of the sloppy burger. He spoke around the mouthful of food. "There aren't a lot of options."

Simon watched the man swipe a thin paper napkin across his mouth and keep chewing.

"I hear there used to be a hole-in-the-wall Mexican place. They tell me the lady who ran it died." Coulter shook his head. "Shame. I love me some Mexican food."

Simon stiffened when the information registered. A Mexican restaurant. The salsa he'd bought was labeled Bonita Anita. Must be a family recipe. The comments Wendell had made about the disposition of Lori's aunt's house all clicked into place.

"Too bad," he managed to reply, keeping his tone detached and unconcerned. The last thing he wanted was Coulter picking up a vibe on how much he was into the town deputy. "This town could use another place to eat. It's either here, or I pick up one of the prepared salads from the Piggly Wiggly."

Coulter took a giant slurp from his disposable cup of sweet tea. He raised the burger, eyeing the dripping mass for where to strike next. "Never could be a salad guy," Coulter said with a wrinkle of his nose. "Rabbit food."

The man took another enormous bite out of the burger, and miraculously, not one speckle of wayward condiment marred the pristine white linen of his shirt. Simon wanted to hate him for aesthetic reasons alone.

"There's a bar out on the highway past my place. Gotta go beyond the interstate ramp to see it. They have a barbecue joint attached," Coulter offered. "They do burnt ends."

Simon inclined his head. "I'll keep it in mind. Thanks." He pulled one of the frilled toothpicks from a triangle of sandwich, took a deep breath and plunged in. "I'm sure you're wondering why I wanted to meet today," he began tentatively.

Coulter shrugged and continued chomping down on his burger. "No problem," he said through stuffed cheeks. "I was going to come see you anyway."

Simon straightened, his senses on high alert. A part of him hoped Coulter was coming to see him to fire him. "Oh? How come?"

Coulter gulped down his food. "Yeah, well, first of all, I got a ticket on the way into town. I'll need you to take care of it for me. Illegal speed trap or something along those lines," he said dismissively. "I saw the pretty lady deputy sitting out by my place, and sure enough, the sheriff was waiting for me the minute I hit the city limits."

"A ticket?"

He took another sip from his cup, flashing Simon a wide, engaging smile. "I guess I didn't take my foot off the accelerator in time to slow down to the posted in-town speed limit." He shrugged. "I'm pretty sure they were tag teaming me. Surely you can find some technicality to get me out of it. I don't mind paying the ticket, but I do mind being trapped."

Simon's heart sank. He had no doubt he could argue his way out of a traffic ticket for the man, even if he didn't particularly want to. "I'll see what I can do. Listen, I wanted to talk to you about one of the guys who works for you."

"Who?" Coulter asked, unconcerned.

"A guy named Rick Dale?"

Coulter pulled a paper sleeve of french fries from his bag. "What about him?"

"He's, uh, a person of interest in the search for a missing girl." Simon watched the other man carefully, scanning for any flicker of complicity.

Coulter's eyes narrowed. "Why do I have a feeling this is going to come back around on me?"

Not wanting to get the man's back up, Simon raised both hands to placate him. "Nope. Not at all. You can't be held responsible for your employee's actions. Does he live on your property?"

"No."

Simon nodded. "Didn't think so." As Coulter's attorney, he was glad to confirm there was no probable cause to search the man's property. As a human being, he was terrified for a sixteen-year-old girl named Jasmine.

"Can you give me an address for him? The girl is underage and—"

To his utter surprise, Coulter dropped his burger and pulled out his phone. "I'll do you one better." Pressing his phone to his ear, he scowled at his cheeseburger. "Dale? It's Coulter. Listen, I don't want to nose around in your life, but I have a half-dozen people who can't seem to find anything better to do but snoop into mine, so I'm only gonna say this once. If there's a girl named Jasmine with you, you need to haul her behind straight home. The girl is jailbait, and if you aren't smart enough to know what that means, I don't need you workin' for me anymore. Got it?" There was a pause. Coulter shook his head hard. "Nope. Don't wanna hear a word. If she's there with you, take her home now and pray her daddy doesn't press charges. Or worse, come after you with a shotgun."

He ended the call. "There. Done." He tucked his phone back into his pocket, shaking his head in disgust. "Man, these kids. They have no idea there's a world of difference between the age of seventeen and eighteen."

Simon gaped at him. "She was there?"

"I have no idea," Coulter said, opening his eyes wide in a parody of innocence. "I didn't ask."

Buoyed by the initial success, Simon straightened and braced himself to approach the next thing he wanted to discuss. "Listen, I've been thinking—"

Coulter held up a hand to stop him. "Wait. I almost forgot the other thing I wanted to tell you. I have another box coming tomorrow. You need to sign for it."

"Tomorrow?" Simon repeated stupidly. "Why are you having a box delivered to me tomorrow? Won't you be in town?"

"I have to be up in Atlanta for a meeting." He plucked a fry from the paper sleeve, bit the end off, then used the rest of the potato to point at Simon. "I told my guy it was okay to direct it to you."

Simon didn't even want to ask who his guy was or what his guy did. "I shouldn't be accepting packages for you."

"I think it's the least you can do for all the money I'm paying you. How hard is it to sign your name?" he asked, giving Simon a hard stare.

There was something sinister in the way the man spoke the words *sign your name*. It made Simon's skin crawl. It gave him the courage to forge ahead. "I'm afraid I won't be able to continue as your attorney. I'm not comfortable with signing for parcels for you, and don't feel I can provide you with an adequate and unbiased defense," he said stiffly. "I'm hoping we can part ways amicably. I'm happy to give you some referrals to other attorneys in nearby towns, or even in Atlanta."

When Simon dared to meet the man's eyes, he realized this was not going to be a simple matter of a frank discussion.

Coulter smiled while he picked up a napkin and meticulously wiped his fingertips. It was the closed-lipped curve of the mouth. The smile of a snake. Simon wanted to look away from his disturbing amber eyes. He didn't want to be ensnared by this man's insidious charm. He feared being crushed by him inch by inch. He'd never been big on the out-doorsy stuff, but he'd hunted enough to sense when something dangerous was coming at you, you didn't dare look away.

"You think I don't know attorneys in Atlanta?" the man asked, clearly amused.

Simon willed himself not to react.

"You think I didn't come to you, Simon Wingate, on purpose?" Coulter said, enunciating every sylla-ble of Simon's name with disdain. "You think I did an internet search for 'attorneys near me' and your name popped up?"

Simon spotted the flat calculation in the man's eyes and dropped his gaze, preparing himself to receive a good lashing from Coulter's forked tongue. What he should have been anticipating were the man's fangs.

"I know who you are, Simon. I know who your daddy is, and your granddaddy too." Coulter picked up another fry and popped it into his mouth, rocking back as he chewed. "I know your hopes and dreams. I know where and when you failed. I know about every mistake you've made, Wingate. Particularly every time you've tripped over the line onto the wrong side of the law," he drawled. "So you got off with a slap on the wrist and a suggestion you leave town for a while. Doesn't mean your past screwups just disappear." He snapped his fingers. "How's your granddaddy's campaign coming? You funnel any of that committee money into it before they caught you tossing out contributions like candy?"

"Listen—"

"No, you listen," Coulter hissed.

Simon steeled himself to meet the man's disturbing gaze.

"I. Picked. You."

A cold flash of horror raced through Simon's bloodstream as the man's words sank in.

"I picked you because you're the man I need on my side. A man with ambition and aspirations. A man with much to lose."

Simon refused to react to the man's implication. "What do you mean? Whether I choose to represent you or not has nothing to do with my father or my grandfather or whatever aspirations I may have in the future."

Coulter simply laughed. "You have absolutely no idea who you're dealing with, do you?"

Simon played the innocent. "I don't understand why we're going down this road at all. It's not like we've had a long-standing relationship. We're not friends. What's your attachment to having me be your attorney?"

Cool and collected, Coulter picked up another fry and dredged it through the small mountain of ketchup he'd squirted onto a pile of napkins. "Missing the point, Wingate. I chose you," he repeated.

Frustrated, Simon shook his head. "I didn't have to take you on."

"But you did." Coulter popped the fry into his mouth and chewed, his gaze impenetrable.

"You're acting like I had no option. I could've said no."

"You could have, but I knew you wouldn't." Coulter plucked a fresh napkin off the pile by his elbow. He wiped his fingers, balled it up and tossed it at Simon's chest.

Simon stared down at the wadded napkin, wondering how the hell he'd stepped into this mess. He'd never been the kid who was picked on in school, nor had he been the bully. He'd been the one who stood on the sidelines disapproving, but doing nothing to stop things from happening to other kids.

Simon wasn't a man inclined to allow himself to be pushed around. He'd never thought himself to be complicit in his silence, but now he felt it. Wiping his damp palms on his pants, he focused on keeping his breaths slow and even. He was too smart to pick a fight with a bully. Coulter's resources far outstripped his, and if he were prepared to make good on his veiled threats, there could be repercussions from this confrontation and they would impact more than himself. So Simon chose to stand down. He wasn't about to be run over.

Holding up his hands in mock surrender, he said, "Whoa. This conversation is escalating to a place it doesn't need to go. I'm only saying I don't intend to keep practicing law here in Pine Bluff for much longer, and I think it might be better for you to find somebody who can handle your needs on a more long-term basis."

Coulter picked up his burger, peeled back the wrapper to expose more of the loaded sandwich and smirked at Simon. "I understand you're only here temporarily, but our relationship can go on even after you leave Pine Bluff. You see, my business interests are wide and varied, and I pay well to have those interests…protected. Seems the occasional favor shouldn't be too much to ask."

He paused long enough to take another outsize bite. Simon waited patiently while the man chomped the food into submission. When he swallowed, he looked across the table, his expression once again flat and unflinching.

"I'm having a box delivered to your office tomorrow, Simon. Express, early delivery. You'll sign for it, and I'll pick it up when I get back to town tomorrow evening." He tapped the table with two fingers, commanding Simon's attention. "Oh, and this is definitely one package you're not going to want to handle."

Without another word, Coulter balled up the remainder of his burger and tossed it into the paper sack. Snagging his fries and tea in one hand, he climbed off the picnic bench and pulled his keys from the pocket of his pants.

"Thanks for lunch. I'll call you when I'm ready to swing by tomorrow."

Simon sat frozen while the man walked away without a backward glance. He flinched when the Viper's powerful engine roared to life. Feeling gut-punched, he stared at the trash Coulter had left strewed across the table.

Another mess for Simon to clean up.

He sat still, waiting for Coulter to pull out and take off. When the roar of the engine faded, Simon closed the lid on his box and swallowed a pang of regret. He'd never order one of the Daisy's mile-high clubs again. And he'd forever resent Samuel Coulter for ruining the silly joke for him.

BACK IN HIS office five minutes later, Simon put a call through to his father. This time when it went to voice mail, he left a message. "Dad, it's me. I need to schedule some time to talk to you tonight. It's important. We may need to conference granddad in on the call too." He paused a minute, trying to think of what else he might need to say. At last, he settled on a simple "I'm sorry. I think I may have screwed up again."

Ending the call, Simon rocked back in the oversize leather executive chair and covered his eyes with crossed forearms. His whole life, he'd wanted to stand out. To not be the third Wendell but to be the only Simon. Now he was coming to realize if he was going to distinguish himself in any way among the Wingate men, it would probably be as the family screwup.

The realization gnawed him. He was not a stupid man. He had ambition, and sometimes it blinded him. He was competent in his skills and comfortable in his own world. Were those bad things? No. If he could remember them here, where he was a fish out of water. Maybe he could figure out a way to snare Samuel Coulter without compromising his own ethics.

Lifting his phone again, he scrolled until he found

the contact information he'd taken from Lori's business card. When the call connected, he spoke with a quiet urgency.

"Will you come to my house tonight?" he asked when she answered. There was a pause on the other end, and he threw himself into it. "I need to talk to you."

"Why me?" Lori Cabrera asked.

"Because we want the same thing."

"We do?"

"Yes." He decided he needed to put forth something in a show of good faith. "And, Lori?"

"Yes?"

"I think… I mean, I hope, uh… Jasmine should be home soon."

"What? How? What are you saying?"

Simon shook his head. "I can't answer those questions. All I can tell you is—"

"Hang on. I have another call," she interrupted. "It's Lena. Hang on."

Simon gripped his phone hard. He was about to disconnect when a breathless Lori came back on the line. "Simon?"

"I'm here."

"Jas is home."

"I'm glad," he said, the words flowing out of him on an exhalation.

"I don't know what you did, but—"

"I didn't do anything," he insisted.

There was a beat of silence. "I'll be over at five thirty," Lori said at last.

Chapter Thirteen

She strode up his front walkway, unsure exactly what she was going to say to Simon. She'd spent two hours at the Joneses' house. At first, Jasmine had been unspeakably sassy and belligerent. Lori had hardly recognized the girl. She was glad she'd refused Lena's request to go along. Lori wasn't sure she wanted her baby sister to witness the rapidly escalating power struggle between Jasmine and her parents.

Rick Dale had been smart enough to drop the girl in front of her house before he hightailed. Smart thinking, as Jasmine's daddy was a former University of Georgia lineman. The scrawny guy she'd seen at the Reptile Rendezvous would be the equivalent of snapping a toothpick. The Joneses were so relieved to see their precious girl they hardly noticed Jasmine's sour attitude.

At first.

Lori followed Jasmine to her bedroom. There, she heard all the expected complaints. They were in love. No one understood. She wasn't a baby.

It took Lori a full thirty minutes and a whole lot of

nodding and humming her sympathy. She graciously refrained from pointing out how quickly her beloved had bailed on her. Finally, the girl worked herself around to admitting she'd been scared to stay with Rick overnight. In talking it all through, Lori was able to ascertain the couple hadn't "gone all the way." Jasmine claimed she told him she wasn't ready, and he loved her enough to respect her wishes. Plus, his bed kind of stank. And his apartment was "gross." He had a roommate named Justin who gave her the creeps, and she didn't mind coming home much. But she loved Rick, and Rick loved her, and she was only staying at her parents' house because the sheets and towels smelled better.

In the end, Lori was convinced Jasmine had scared herself.

Now she was anxious to see Simon Wingate. Maybe even a little scared. She wanted to talk with him, maybe try to talk some sense into him in regard to Samuel Coulter if she could. She wanted to stop sparring with him and air out all this unspoken tension between them once and for all.

"Hɪ," ʜᴇ sᴀɪᴅ as he answered the doorbell. "Come in."

"Hi. I was surprised to get your call, but I guess you heard that Jasmine is home again," she said, shoving her fingers into her jeans pockets and giving a lopsided shrug. "I heard your client made a phone call. Thank you."

"Don't thank me yet," he said, his expression grim. "I need to talk to you."

Lori heard the apprehension in his statement and proceeded with equal caution. "Okay. What do you need to talk to me about?"

"Please sit."

They chose seats on opposite ends of the sofa, but Lori noted how he turned his body to face her directly, and she liked it. She wanted to put all their bickering aside. She didn't know him well, but, aside from his tastes in clientele, what she did know, she liked. Probably more than she wanted to admit.

Simon inhaled deeply and he tipped his head back to stare at the ceiling. "I need you to bear with me while I talk this out in a way which won't get me disbarred," he said quietly.

"Disbarred?"

"I'm having some issues with a few things about a client," he said, choosing each word carefully. "Of course, most of my interactions with this client are bound by attorney-client privilege." He paused and cast his eyes to the ceiling. "Hey, did I tell you I'm also being subtly blackmailed?" he asked, keeping his tone light and casual.

His eyes met hers and held. She sucked in a short breath, but played along. "No. Are you? I didn't think people were blackmailed outside of the movies."

He nodded. "All the time. You see it a lot in politics." He stared, prompting her to read between the lines.

Politics. Someone was threatening to hurt his family politically. Someone who was a client. A client with enough money and clout to hurt the Wingate family's political prospects in some way.

Samuel Coulter.

Lori pressed the tips of her fingers to her lips to keep from speaking the man's name aloud. She didn't want to do anything to cause Simon to shut down their conversation. She offered a wobbly smile as she parsed through various ways of approaching the problem.

"Okay, well, wow. Puts a new spin on things, does it?"

"Yes, it does."

"So, uh, I'm not sure what the bounds of attorney-client privilege are exactly," she began.

"They cover pretty much everything, unless, of course, a client decides to tell someone who is not their attorney, or the client uses the attorney's services to commit a crime or fraud."

"Has your client done either of those things?"

"Not to my knowledge," he responded, speaking with enough deliberate care to make it clear something may have been done without his explicit knowledge.

"Wow. Okay. Complicated. How about I ask some questions and maybe you can answer them if you can or tell me if you can't?"

Simon nodded. "Might work."

"Okay." She gave a laugh. "I never thought I'd be the one asking questions. You're the lawyer, not me."

He gave a wry smile. "I bet you're pretty good at asking questions all on your own."

"All right. I guess we'll kind of begin with some

random stuff to warm up." She paused and tried to come up with the most innocuous question she could think up. "Is your first name actually Wendell?"

He laughed. "Absolutely. Telling women my name is Wendell does nothing to benefit my cause."

"It has a certain nerdish charm," she allowed. "Tell me, are you presently retained to represent a man named Samuel Coulter?"

"Yes." Simon punctuated the admission with a brisk nod.

"Does this conversation have anything to do with a particular client?"

He pursed his lips, considering the question from all angles. "I don't think I can answer one way or another."

"Fair enough." Lori ticked the yes column on her mental score sheet.

"Do you believe one of your clients may be engaged in criminal activity?"

Simon beamed a smile at her, but he shook his head. "I can't answer directly. Calls for speculation. I have seen no evidence of criminal activity, but I think we can make a general assumption at least one of my clients has allegedly engaged in some questionable, if not criminal, behavior."

"Okay, so if I were to invite Ben over here for a beer, and he and I were to have a conversation about all of our suspicions about all of the people who may or may not be doing things of a criminal nature here in Masters County, is there any way you could point us in the right direction?"

This time Simon laughed. "You went way too broad in your questioning. Granddad used to say, 'You catch a lot of little fish with a big net, but you need a strong hook to snag the big ones.' You were on track. Stick with specifics where you can."

"Okay, well, I'm not the one who wanted to talk without doing any talking," she retorted tartly.

He inclined his head in acquiescence. "Understood." He tapped his fingers on his denim-clad knee. "I hear Ben had a friend from the DEA visit," he asked in a studiedly casual tone that made the fine hairs on her arm ripple.

She hesitated, watching him carefully. "Yes. Why do you ask?"

He shrugged. "Curious, is all. Were they stopping by to say hello, or was there a purpose in coming here?"

Lori frowned, uncertain how much she should disclose to this man. After all, he was representing the man Special Agent Simmons had come to Masters County to investigate. Maybe his whole come-over-and-talk thing was a ruse. Perhaps she'd read the situation tragically wrong.

Her mind racing with possibilities, she answered, "I can't comment on that."

Simon blew out a breath. "Okay, so we both have things we can't talk about." He studied her intently. "I am going to assume if the DEA has business in Pine Bluff, it has nothing to do with any of my clients."

She gave an overly hearty laugh to signal he was way off base without saying the words.

"Or maybe it does," he amended, speaking slowly.

"Only one of my clients has had any difficulty lately, and nothing I am aware of would fall under the purview of the Drug Enforcement Administration. Unless you're going to try to convince me Timmy Showalter is a bigger fish than I thought."

"No. Timmy's nothing more than a kid who doesn't make good choices."

"I'm trying to figure out what the issue might be," he pressed.

"The issue is, you can't talk about whatever it is that's eating at you, so we're sitting here talking in circles." She tossed up her hands in frustration. "What am I doing here?"

Moving closer to her on the sofa, he said, "Lori, I'm not the bad guy here."

"I know," she whispered, touched by the raw vulnerability in his plea.

"Do you?" he asked, leaning in closer to peer into her eyes. "I really want you to believe me."

"I do."

"Okay," he whispered, almost to himself. "I have a lot of thinking to do, and I need to talk to my dad and Wendell about some stuff, but I wanted you to—" he slanted her a rueful smile "—keep an open mind about me."

"Okay," she agreed, breathless.

"I wish this was easier."

The rasp in his voice was enough to make her believe him. "You wish what was easier?"

"You and me."

"You and me?" she asked, stunned, but pleased by his directness.

"Yes. I want things to be easier between you and me."

She found herself caught up in his intense stare. "You do?"

"Yes. I want to be...with you, but I also want to feel like a man who deserves to be with you."

"And you don't think you are?"

His laugh was short but genuine. "You've spent the past couple of weeks reminding me I'm slime like my client."

"True," she murmured.

She gave him a playful once-over, mainly because she was unable to look him straight in the eye. Her entire life, she'd been taught there were only two sides to every coin. Right and wrong. Truth or lies. Grace and sin. Now she found herself seated on a squishy sofa across from a man she wanted more than she cared to admit, and staring into a giant gray abyss. She wanted him. He wanted her. That was the truth.

"Lori—"

"You're right. This is complicated."

"I'm working on uncomplicating things. The problem is, there's more at stake here than me or you or what either of us might want."

"Okay," she replied. Her desire to push or cajole him into stepping out of the dark and into the light was immediately subdued by the earnest appeal. So she asked the only question she had left. "Then what can I do to help?"

Chapter Fourteen

After extracting a promise from Lori not to give up on him and asking her to stand by as he figured out a way to wriggle out from under Coulter's thumb, Simon showed Lori to the door.

Thirty minutes later, he had both his father and grandfather conferenced in on a call. Once he brought his father up to speed regarding Samuel Coulter, Simon told them about their lunch meeting and the not-so-veiled threats Coulter issued.

His grandfather broke in. "So he's implying he has the means to damage your political prospects."

"Not only mine," Simon said morosely. "All of ours."

There was a beat of silence. At last, his father spoke up. "The man can't possibly have anything on me. I've done nothing wrong." Dell paused and Simon could conjure his earnest, thoughtful expression in his mind's eye. "To the best of my knowledge, I've never met him. I think it's an empty threat. The man is operating under the general impression all politicians have something to hide."

"I concur," Wendell said gravely. "I did handle the sale of his land, but I was the seller's attorney. He used some fellow out of Miami, Florida, for his end of the transaction."

"He seems to have a lot of ties to Miami," Simon mused. "I've looked into his business ventures, but they appear to be on the up-and-up. At least, on the surface. Made his initial fortune day-trading and expanded from there. Owns real estate all over Florida, a few small businesses, but nothing to bring in the big money. From what I can see, he made the bulk of it in the stock market."

"At least the part of it that's aboveboard." Wendell gave a dismissive sniff. "You wouldn't find any evidence of illegal activities online, would you?"

"No," Simon admitted. "The snake thing is pretty out there. People with money can sometimes go wacky with it, but this appears to be a lifelong obsession."

"I can go back through whatever wildlife legislation I've voted on in the last couple of sessions, but I honestly can't think of any way in which our mutual interests may have crossed paths," Dell concluded.

"Which leaves Simon," Wendell said gravely. "He said he picked you. I'm with your dad in thinking he threw us into the mix for some extra oomph. Your activities on behalf of the natural gas consortium's political action committee weren't a state secret. He probably thinks he can twist your arm harder by adding us in for good measure."

Though it had been nearly a year since Simon had

accidentally jeopardized his entire political future by not doing his due diligence on behalf of his lobbying firm, he couldn't argue with his grandfather's conclusion. What Simon had done hadn't been illegal, but the optics weren't good. He'd taken the fall for the firm, walking away with not much more than an unspoken promise of their future support in his back pocket. Now he wasn't certain he wanted to get into the game at all.

"Yeah." He drew a shaky breath. "I admit he threw me at first, but now I can't help but think he's playing chicken with me."

"Good analogy," Wendell said with a chuckle. "Ye gods, son, what did you think the man could possibly have on your father or me?"

"I have no clue," Simon replied honestly. "You're the one who keeps telling me dangerous creatures lurk in these woods. You're the one who told me I needed to come here and take on some easy lawyering while I waited for people to get forgetful. Now I'm trapped in Pine Bluff with this guy using me."

"I did tell you those things," Wendell admitted ruefully. "I didn't tell you to take Coulter on. You chose him. When something too good to be true drops into your lap, it's because it's too good to be true."

Simon bristled when his father piled on.

"Your ego always trips you up, son. You wanted to make a splash. And you wanted to impress this Coulter fellow because he's sittin' on a pile of cash," Dell concluded.

His grandfather picked up the baton again. "Not

saying you've done anything wrong. We've all spent some time cultivating some wealthy and powerful people. The problem is, sometimes you allow yourself to be blinded by flash."

There was a long silence, and in it, Simon read his father's tacit agreement with his grandfather's assessment. It pained him, but Simon couldn't say it wasn't true. His whole life, all he wanted was to step into the Wingate legacy. The problem was, every time he took a chance and tried to set himself apart from his father and grandfather, he ended up tripping and falling flat on his face.

He was ruminating on this when his father spoke up.

"There are ways for you to be able to off-load him, but sacrifices may have to be made on your part. More risk taken."

Simon scoffed. "You mean possibly jeopardizing my entire political future. Let's face it—my chances are already slim. With the campaign contribution mess and whatever it is I've gotten myself into down here aside, no one is going to elect an attorney who has been disbarred."

"There are always ways to spin unsavory items from our past into more palatable chunks for public consumption," Wendell insisted. "It comes back to the best defense being a good offense. We need to figure out a way for you to get out ahead of this guy, if not out from under him."

There was another long pause. He could almost

hear the three of them pondering different angles. At last, his grandfather chimed in.

"Dora tells me there's a new lady in town. She's supposedly gone to work at Timber Masters," Wendell commented mildly.

"I clearly need to find more for Dora to do if she has time to report every scrap of local gossip back to you," Simon replied. "Of course, keeping her occupied will be much harder if I ditch my neediest client."

"It's a catch-22," Wendell agreed with a hum. "Aside from her ability to keep an ear to the ground, Dora is an excellent judge of people."

"She is," Dell said. "She told me I was going to propose to your mother five minutes after she met her."

Wendell let loose with a guffaw. "Well, son, anyone with eyes in their head could see you were smitten. The bigger question was whether Bettina would have you."

"Can we get back to the subject at hand?" Simon asked, impatient with the conversational detour.

"We're still on the subject," his grandfather replied mildly. "Dora says this woman looks like a Fed."

The three men fell silent.

After digesting the information, Simon spoke up. "I was about to ask how Dora might know how to tag a federal agent, but then I remembered where I am."

"Mmm-hmm," Wendell hummed. "If anyone's going to be able to spot a Fed a mile away, it's Dora. She watched me go toe-to-toe with enough of them."

"Funny, Ben Kinsella had a friend from the DEA come to town earlier this week," Simon informed them.

"Did he now?" Wendell mused. "Isn't that interesting. I didn't think he'd left on the best of terms with many of his colleagues there."

"Do you think there's trafficking happening in the area?" Dell asked.

"The only thing I've come across was a teenager caught with some weed," Simon informed them.

"There's worse going on," Wendell said ominously. "I think it may behoove you to have a frank conversation with our friends over in the law and justice center."

"And say what? 'Hey, I think my client might be a bad guy after all'?" Simon demanded.

"Did I say you should speak to them about your client?" Wendell retorted, the question uncharacteristically sharp. "I said you should sit down with some of your friends and neighbors. Be a part of the community. Try having your finger on the pulse rather than one foot out the door."

His grandfather's impatience came through loud and clear. Simon ducked his head, tensing his jaw to keep from snapping back. Because, damn it, the old man was right.

"Your granddad is right," Dell said calmly, ever the peacemaker. "You think my trips back home are duty visits to maintain support, but you're wrong. Chet Rinker and I have been best friends since nursery school. Your mother pretends she's jealous Trudy Skyler and I went steady in the eleventh grade, but

I think she does it to make me feel good. I'm on the alumni homecoming committee, and not so I can ride in the parade. Pine Bluff is my home," he said, his voice conveying a depth of feeling microphones never quite got across.

"Your mama is an Atlanta girl. She'd never have been happy living in such a small town full-time, so I made some sacrifices. Maybe I should have put my foot down more when you were coming up, but if you hope to represent those people one day, you need to know who they are and what they need."

The simple truth of what his father and grandfather were saying hit him hard. The thing Lori had said about him thinking he was too cool for this place ping-ponged around in his head. They weren't wrong. He'd been resisting settling in. Refusing to believe his time in Pine Bluff was anything more than a speed bump in his life. His chest felt tight and his head too heavy to hold up. Shame pulsed through his veins and warmed his skin.

"You're right," he said at last.

"What did you say?" Wendell prodded. "Can you repeat that?"

"Dad, don't," Dell said preemptively. When Wendell refrained from further commentary, Simon's father pressed on. "It's a good suggestion, Simon. Maybe something more like a meeting," he mused. "A few key people and some frank discussion."

"Yes. A breakfast meeting," Wendell suggested. "Perhaps around the time your express deliveries usually show up."

"Good idea," Dell chimed in effusively. "Never hurts to have a few witnesses around too."

"Hey, did I tell you I ran into Roy Biddle the other day?" Wendell asked Dell.

While his father and grandfather swapped stories about the people they'd run into on their separate campaigns, Simon tapped out a text message.

I need a favor.

He waited, inserting cursory grunts and the expected laughs at intervals. At last, the ellipses indicating a reply was being typed appeared.

Yes?

Can you convince Ben and Harry to meet with us at my office tomorrow morning around 7 or 7:30?

Lori's reply came less than a minute later.

No problem with Ben, but I'll have to check with Harry. You lawyers keep far more leisurely hours. What's up?

He smiled as he listened to his father complain about the number of Auburn fans who'd shown up at his last town hall meeting. Thumbs flying, he typed.

I need to get some perspective on some things. Tell the guys I'll provide coffee and doughnuts.

Always a good incentive. She added an emoji of someone drooling. See you in the a.m.

Simon grinned and tuned back in to the conversation in time to hear Wendell spout off about the "overopinionated knuckleheads" who called into his favorite sports talk-radio station. He couldn't help thinking things were looking up.

THERE WAS NOTHING but a box of doughnuts between him and the woman he wanted to kiss again. Well, the doughnuts, the massive oak conference table, the district attorney and Sheriff Ben Kinsella, who'd eyed him with wary suspicion when he and Lori exchanged greetings notably warmer than they'd been when they'd convened in the judge's chambers.

Though he had no chance of getting "more kissing" added to the morning's agenda, so far his new friends and neighbors had been nothing but forthcoming in giving him their take on the current state of affairs in Masters County.

"You can probably get actual data from the state agencies," Ben was saying. "I can tell you things on the ground have been shifting." He bit into his second cream-filled doughnut and sighed. "I wish I didn't love these things so much. I hate being a cliché."

Lori snickered, and Ben shot her a warning glance. Simon fought the urge to smile reflexively when she hid her own.

"Opioids," Hayes announced, jerking him back to the conversation at hand. "The stuff that went down last spring with the killings associated with Jared

Baker and the Crystal Forest Corporation fronting methamphetamine production slowed some of the meth trade in the area, but nature abhors a vacuum. When the crystal wasn't readily available, people started raiding medicine cabinets."

"Rinker's Pharmacy has been broken into no less than three times in the past year," Lori informed him. "Of course, they can't get to anything valuable. Mr. Rinker has his place fortified better than a Pentagon bunker."

Simon scoffed. "You're kidding."

Without missing a beat, Lori spoke to Ben, her expression completely blank. "Simon thinks I'm the funniest woman he's ever met," she said in a voice devoid of inflection. "Whenever I say something, all he ever says is 'You're kidding.' He thinks everything I say is a joke."

"No. Not at all," Simon interjected, scooting to the edge of his seat, ready to talk his way out of whatever circular argument she wanted to invent. "I was simply using a phrase commonly used to express shock and disbelief."

"He doesn't believe a word I say," she said blandly.

"I believe your every utterance to be the gospel truth. I'm the one with limited capacity," he said dryly.

"Addiction to opiates has been on the rise throughout the country," the DA continued, shooting Ben and Lori an exasperated glance. "I'm sure you've heard on the news," he added. "Rural areas are particularly hard-hit because the supply isn't steady. The ebb and flow can lead to people doing some pretty desperate things."

"Tighter restrictions on making prescription meds available for recreational use has led people to look for alternatives," Ben said, his expression grave.

Simon glanced from face to face, slotting all the pieces together. "So you're saying there is a trafficking problem in the area," he concluded.

"We're saying we have reason to believe there is," Ben clarified.

"Now we're not only looking for methamphetamine," Hayes said grimly, "but also heroin."

Simon found himself holding his breath, wondering for the millionth time how he'd stumbled into this predicament. His path had been laid out for him since he was a boy. Okay, so he'd tried to take a shortcut and ended up sidelined, but his push for power hadn't knocked him out of the game completely. Coming to Pine Bluff was supposed to be the safe bet, but he'd rolled snake eyes on his initial pass. Now he had to find a way to indicate he'd be open to helping them find whatever it was they suspected.

"I watched that show everyone's been talking about last night. *Exotic Escapades*? The one on Cineflix about the people who claim to do exotic-animal rescue," Ben said, his conversation casual yet oddly pointed. When their eyes met, the sheriff smiled wide and affably. "Have y'all watched it?"

Lori shook her head and Harry simply snorted, but Ben paid no attention to them. His gaze was locked on Simon.

"No," Simon said, approaching the conversational gambit with caution. "I've heard it's a hot mess, though. Doesn't seem your type of thing."

Ben nodded. "It's not, but Alicia Simmons was telling us all about it at dinner last night."

Simon felt all three sets of eyes boring into him. They were testing him. Or trying to tell him something without actually speaking the words out loud. So he swung at the softball Ben had lobbed at him. "Alicia Simmons? I don't think I've had the pleasure of meeting her yet."

Ben rocked back in his chair, his gaze so steady, Simon was beginning to wonder if there was a red laser dot at the center of his forehead.

"She's new to town. Coming down from Atlanta to work for Marlee in inventory control over at Timber Masters," the man said, the picture of casualness.

"No wonder the name didn't register for me." Simon did his best not to let his confusion show. He suspected Ben was steering this conversation in a particular direction, and he was willing to go along for the ride. "From Atlanta, huh?"

"Yep. I believe she was born and raised in the area," Ben continued.

The silence stretched for a few heartbeats. Simon got the feeling he was supposed to respond to this information, but he didn't have the first clue how or why. "I can't say the name is familiar to me, but Atlanta isn't Pine Bluff, is it? I swear, I can't remember the last time I ran into anyone born and bred up there."

Ben laced his fingers together and rocked forward in his chair until his hands landed on the table with a soft thunk. "I knew her some when I lived there."

Framed as it was, the admission shocked Simon. Was this Alicia Simmons the mysterious friend from the Drug Enforcement Administration? If so, what was she doing coming to work at Timber Masters? Unless—

"From your time with the DEA?" he asked bluntly, tired of the subterfuge.

The corners of Ben's mouth curved upward in a smile. "Yep."

"Wow. Well, talk about an interesting career transition." Simon shifted his gaze between Lori and Hayes. Neither of them seemed to be surprised or impressed by the morning's revelations. "I take it she's here temporarily?"

"I believe so," Ben replied so casually they could have been speculating about the weather.

Simon simply nodded. "Okay."

Another awkward silence descended on the room.

Hayes sat up too, making a show of checking the time on his wristwatch. Ben shifted in his seat. Rumpled and unshaven, the sheriff had clearly come off an overnight shift. "Well, I appreciate the sunrise breakfast, but I—"

"Wait," Simon blurted, startling his three guests.

When they looked at him, puzzlement and suspicion written all over their faces, he felt a hot flash of embarrassment. For a man trained to win oral arguments, he was having a hard time keeping his guests interested enough to hang around until the damn express delivery van got around to him.

"I, uh…" He cast about, hoping to find another topic compelling enough to keep them seated for a few more minutes. "About Coulter…"

He clammed up and stared back at their expectant faces. What the hell was he going to say? They waited, their expressions a tossed salad of wariness, expectation and caution. Thankfully, the front door burst open and Dora bustled into the foyer, speaking loudly enough to draw everyone's attention away from him.

"No. I will not sign my name," she was saying, her voice sharp and precise. "I am not Mr. Coulter's representative… Simon!"

He flinched when she bellowed his name. The other three swiveled in their seats, their attention fixed on the door to the conference room. Launching from his chair, he did his best to keep his voice light and cajoling, hoping a laugh would cover his nerves. What he was about to do could backfire in his face, but he had to do something.

"Yes, ma'am," he said, hurrying toward the reception area. "I'm in a meeting, Dora." He drew to a stop at the conference room door. "What's wrong?"

"You've got another box of snakes." She complained so loudly, Simon wanted to hug her. "I thought you told him you weren't going to accept any more packages on his behalf."

Smirking, Simon stepped into the foyer. A shipping box nearly twice the size of the last one sat at the feet of a uniformed delivery driver. The man practically threw the electronic tablet at Simon.

"I need a signature," he said with a hint of desperation.

"Of course." Simon took the stylus the man offered and scrawled his name in the signature window. "Thank you." The man took his tablet back and scuttled out the front door.

Pitching his voice loud enough for the people in the next room to hear, he said, "I did inform our client we did not wish to accept any additional packages on his behalf, but he told me this one was already in transit and reminded me he has our firm on retainer to act on his behalf."

"Doesn't make you his errand boy," Dora snapped.

"No," Simon replied, dropping his voice to a more intimate level. "It means he has a certain amount of say in the services he expects me to provide for him." He pulled his phone from his pocket and started snapping photos of the box. "You go on and settle in. I'll finish up in here."

Dora jerked her chin toward the conference room. "Who are you meeting with so early?"

"It's Harrison Hayes, Ben Kinsella and Lori Cabrera," he said, slipping the phone back into his pocket. He eyed the box, mentally psyching himself up to lift it.

"You should tell them what he's been shipping in here," she said with a huff.

"It's not illegal," he reminded her, hoisting the box.

Not only was it larger, it was also heavier than the

last. Either the man had a dozen or so baby snakes in there or one fairly large one. He grimaced and held the box away from his body as he carried it into the conference room.

"Sorry," he said, placing the box on the credenza situated parallel to the conference table. The box was clearly marked. He made sure the label was facing them, plain as day. Plastering a smile on his face, he nodded to his guests. "Well, I guess we should all get on with our busy days."

Lori shot him an incredulous look. "Seriously? You took delivery of what appears to be a box of snakes and you don't expect us to ask questions about it?"

"You can ask whatever questions you need to ask," he replied, opening his hands in an invitation for them to bring them on. "Whether I can answer them is a different matter."

"Does that box have what I think it has in it?" she persisted.

"I cannot even pretend to be able to read your mind, Deputy," he said with a placid smile.

"You don't have to ask," Harry pointed out. "It says so right there it's a boa constrictor."

"Yes, I believe they have to label all shipments of live reptiles," Simon informed him.

"I guess we don't have to ask who it's for," Ben said, rising from his seat.

"I can't say, anyway," Simon said, keeping his eyes locked on the sheriff.

"Do your clients regularly ship things to you?" Hayes asked, his gaze sharpening.

"No." Simon shook his head. "Only one client, and it's only been a couple of times when he's been away and unable to accept delivery." He made a point of glancing at the box. "Makes Dora uncomfortable, though, so I'll keep the box in here until my client gets back later today."

Hayes exchanged a glance with Ben.

Lori stared at him, her face a mask of stark disbelief. "You know this guy is up to no good. I can't understand how you can continue to defend him, much less sign your name to packages delivered to him. Doesn't that put you at risk?"

Simon caught the note of worry in her admonishment, and a sort of cool calm washed over him. It was the polar opposite of the heat he felt when he kissed her, but it pleased him all the same. Her worry meant she cared, and if she cared, he could let go of his own worries.

Pulling his phone from his pocket, he waved it at her. "I've taken photos of anything I signed for, so I can show my client the packaging was intact upon delivery and upon transfer to its rightful owner. On the advice of *my* attorney," he added with a sly smile.

"Good thinking." Hayes stood, and Simon watched as the district attorney and the sheriff both made their way around the opposite end of the conference table. They'd pass right by the box on the credenza on their way out, and he wouldn't have to say a word about it.

Lori stayed stubbornly planted, her eyes darting

nervously from Simon to Ben and back again when the two men passed by her. Simon wanted to reach out to her, tell her this was all a part of his plan. Then again, it wasn't much of a plan to brag on.

"Ben, I hear you have a friend who's new to town. Boy, that can be rough around here," Simon said, letting out a low whistle.

The sheriff's step slowed, and he glanced over at Lori, surprise and bewilderment written all over his face. Simon leaped in to save her the trouble of having to answer to her boss. "Marlee mentioned it when we had lunch the other day. Then Dora reported back to Wendell the new lady Marlee hired looked like a Fed." He chuckled. "Anyway, you and I know how hard it can be when you're the new kid in town." He shot a pointed glance at the box, then met the sheriff's steady gaze again. "You should bring her by sometime to introduce her. Maybe this afternoon. I don't have anything going on until my client swings by to get his box."

THE MINUTE THEY left Simon's office, Ben unclipped his phone and started thumbing through the screens. Lori shot Hayes a look. "You get what he's doing, don't you?"

Harrison gave a short nod. "Yep."

"He could get in trouble, couldn't he? I mean, big trouble," she said worriedly. "Last night, he said something about being disbarred."

"He won't be disbarred," Harry answered distractedly. "His client might fire him, file a grievance or

make things difficult for him, but he won't be disbarred. He's playing this smart."

"Not if he wants to have a career in politics," she
answered.

Hayes faced her directly. "Does he? When did he
tell you he did? I got the impression the two of you
didn't exactly trade confidences."

"Alicia's going to come hang out with me this afternoon," Ben announced, ending the call. "I'll take
her around, introduce her to some folks."

"What?" Lori asked, baffled by Ben's willingness
to play along in this murky swamp of a situation.

"Like Simon said," the sheriff answered with a
shrug.

Lori glowered at him, wondering if the sheriff had
lost his mind. "Like Simon said," she hissed, "there's
a boa constrictor in there." She pointed to the door.
"Your friend was the one who told us the DEA suspected Coulter was smuggling drugs using his stupid
snakes," she reminded him, her voice rising.

Ben simply nodded. "Yes, she did. I believe I'll
take her by to meet Simon this afternoon. You never
know who we'll run into while we're there."

Hayes patted her arm reassuringly. "I'll get with
Judge Nichols on the paperwork. We'll need a warrant for the box, once it's in Coulter's custody, and
another for his property, if the contents of the box
give us enough justification."

She and Ben watched the DA hustling toward the
municipal building. "And what am I supposed to do?
Nothing?" Lori demanded.

Ben was a step ahead of her. "I need you to interview both Jasmine Jones and Kaylin Bowers, but this time, focus on the snakes. I hate to say this, but I almost think all this stuff he and his guys were pulling with the young girls in the area was sort of a smoke screen. You said yourself Dale didn't do anything with Jasmine Jones sexually."

Lori noted the flush darkening the sheriff's cheeks. "No. She said he didn't try anything."

"Exactly," Ben said, jabbing a finger at her. "What nineteen-year-old guy doesn't try to get it on with the girl he's been flirting with? Those guys knew better. If anyone is good at tightrope walking the law, it's Coulter. Hell, he could have terrorized and dumped Bella Nunes out on the highway hoping someone would pick her up. Like bait."

"Bait?"

"To distract us from what was going on." He paused for a minute. "Maybe call Bella Nunes too. She was the one who got the closest to the snakes themselves."

Lori shuddered, remembering how scared the girl had been the night she'd picked her up on the highway. "Okay, but what do I ask them?"

Ben tipped his head back. "Is this how all the snakes come in? Does he ship any out? You said something about one of the girls meeting a guy at a tent revival. Do they move the snakes in any other way? Do they let people handle them in the park?" He leaned in to look her in the eye. "I need you to lock down your feelings about Simon and Coulter, and think about the bigger picture. Can you do that?"

"Of course I can," she snapped, insulted.

Ben didn't back off. "Good, because I can tell you I wasn't too great about keeping my feelings for Marlee under wraps when her world was blowing up."

Lori could feel Ben's steady gaze boring into her cheekbone. "Okay. Yeah. I get you," she said at last.

"There's no shame in caring about people, Lori, but right now we have an open window and a clear shot," he said gruffly. "We need every scrap of information those girls might have, and you are the best person for extracting it. I need you to look past the smoke screen. We need you sharpshooter focused, because moving or not, the target is the same."

She nodded once. "Right. I'm on it."

Ben clapped her on the shoulder and prodded her toward the office. "Come on."

Lori shook her head. "No. I'm going to have to get parental permission to speak to Kaylin and Jas. I'm going to walk over to the Joneses' right now. They told me they'd be taking a day or two to work things through."

"Okay, good." He hooked his sheriff's department ball cap onto his head and raised a hand in farewell. "Call me with any info. I'll get Alicia in and we'll start going over how we want to approach this."

Lori took about three steps in the opposite direction, then cast a concerned glance at the renovated home where Wendell had long ago established the Wingate Law Firm and Simon fought to keep it alive.

She didn't have time to go back in to see him. It peeved her to think she'd been taken in by Samuel Coulter's smoke and mirrors, but she didn't have time for ego indulgence. Simon had given them this opportunity, and she was determined to make the most of it.

Chapter Fifteen

Simon tried not to fidget under Special Agent Alicia Simmons's unflinching stare, but he was fighting a losing battle. Tall and solid, with a no-nonsense manner, the woman was intimidating.

"I am sure you are aware most of the information Deputy Cabrera collected from the young women who'd been involved with the Reptile Rendezvous or its employees is hearsay and inadmissible, but it does paint a slightly clearer picture. From what we can gather, Coulter uses the reptiles he claims to nurture as little more than snakeskin suitcases."

Simon felt his stomach roll over. "Allegedly," he said quietly.

Special Agent Simmons obligingly added the word. "I'm sorry. Coulter *allegedly* uses his business as a front for moving product coming in from Mexico and Colombia. We believe the primary means of entry to be via cruise ship, but it's not unusual to fly it in." She shared a wan smile with Ben. "Illegal substances coming into the country are usually easier to catch. Distribution, well, that's where we play Whac-A-Mole."

"The DEA believes Samuel Coulter is a much bigger player than his operation here in Georgia would let on," Ben informed him. "He has a number of ways to move product from South Florida. He's sort of a high-level middleman, connecting the larger organizations who import it with existing distribution networks."

Alicia Simmons picked the thread up again. "He has established ties to Jacksonville, Florida, and Atlanta, but we believe he has become the leading supplier feeding the back roads leading up through the Appalachians."

"Doesn't seem there'd be much money in moving it through the mountains," Simon commented with a frown.

"More people get a cut in the cities," Alicia explained with a shrug. "Eastern Tennessee, Kentucky, West Virginia, Ohio… The rural communities in these states have been ravaged by opiate addiction." She leveled a glare at him. "Your client has finally made himself the kingpin he's always wanted to be."

Simon opened his mouth, then closed it again when he felt Ben's hand land heavy on his shoulder.

"You don't have to do a thing, Simon. Let this happen. The plan is in place. The box has been x-rayed, and we know the specimen in it is more than large enough for him to use for transport. When Coulter comes to collect his parcel, the game warden and I will serve him with the warrant and ask him to cut the tape and open the box. If he refuses, we'll ask you to open it as his representative."

A shudder ran through him and Ben must have felt it.

"You only have to cut the tape. Alicia and representatives from the state and US fish and wildlife departments will be on hand. Lori got some good information on the number and kind of snakes coming in and out of there from Kaylin Bowers and Bella Nunes. Enough to persuade Judge Nichols to issue a warrant. Lori and her team are in position to serve the warrant the moment we have Coulter."

Simon hated the thought of Lori charging in armed with nothing more than a piece of paper and whatever backup Alicia Simmons could scare up on short notice. He couldn't help feeling it would take an army to bring down a man like Samuel Coulter.

Simon's phone lit up and Samuel Coulter's name appeared on the display. "Here he is."

Ben nodded to it. "Go ahead."

Simon answered the call, but put his client on speaker so they could all hear. "Hello?"

"Hey, Simon. Got my package?" Coulter asked, his tone jovial.

Irritated, Simon laid it on thick, hoping to come across as conciliatory and eager to please after the previous day's confrontation. "Your box arrived. Miss Dora took one look at the label and made me put it up in the conference room for safekeeping." He chuckled, hoping to establish camaraderie. "You keep shippin' those things here and I'm gonna have to give her a raise. I can barely afford her now," he complained, pouring on the good-old-boy charm he'd inherited from his father and grandfather.

Coulter chuckled. "Do what you have to do. I honestly don't understand why people get so squeamish around serpents. They are the most amazing creatures."

Simon looked up at Ben and Alicia. "To each his or her own."

"Yes, well, I am less than thirty minutes out. I apologize if I keep you at the office a few minutes after five."

"No problem," Simon said, his fake bonhomie sounding hollow to his own ears. "I can certainly hang around awhile."

"I'll be there shortly," Coulter replied.

Simon exhaled when the beeps indicating the end of the call bounced off his office walls. He double-checked the screen. "Well, okay." He checked his watch and was relieved to see it was well past four o'clock. "Okay, so we have an ETA."

Ben called Lori's cell phone directly to relay the information. When he disconnected, Simon frowned at him. "Is she not wearing a radio?"

Ben frowned. "What? Yeah. Of course she is."

"Why did you call her cell?" Simon asked, nodding to the phone Ben gripped in his hand.

"Because people love to listen in on police band radios." Ben shot him a glance. "You'd think they'd teach that in ambulance-chaser school."

Simon rolled his eyes. "I must have been sick that day."

Ben smiled and dropped down into one of the conference room chairs, stretching his bulky frame to fill the space, seemingly relaxed. Simon envied the man's ability to shrug off the stress of this situation. Right now, he felt his skin fit two sizes too small.

"So, what's going on with you two?" Ben asked.

His tone was so offhand Simon knew the question was anything but casual. He didn't have any answers himself. How was he supposed to come up with some for Ben?

"Who two?" he parried.

"You and my deputy," Ben said pointedly.

"I've only met Mike the one time, but he seemed decent enough," Simon replied evenly, unwilling to give himself or Lori away so easily.

"Lori."

The sheriff spoke her name with such gravity, Simon couldn't bring himself to foist the man off with flippancy. "I don't know," he answered honestly.

"You think something is going on," Ben concluded.

Simon gave a jerky nod. "Something is going on."

Silence hung heavy between them, but Simon refused to say anything more on the matter.

"She's had a rough time of it," Ben said at last.

"I am aware," Simon replied quietly.

"And she's not the type to…"

The other man paused, and Simon wondered which of the many facets of his possible relationship with Lori he would choose to object to first.

"She's rooted here," Ben concluded.

"I get it."

"Do you?" The sheriff looked straight at him.

Simon schooled his expression into something neutral. "Yes."

"Okay," Ben answered at last.

Simon snorted, shocked by the laconic response. "'Okay'? All you have to say is 'okay'?"

Ben shrugged. "You're both adults, and I'm not her daddy. I trust Lori to make good decisions. If she decides on you, then she must have thought it through."

When five o'clock came, Dora stood outside the conference room door with her purse caught in the crook of her arm. She looked from Simon to Ben and back again. The tiny lines on her forehead bunched together into one deep crease of worry. "Do you want me to stay?"

Simon shook his head. "It would be better if you didn't. We need to make everything seem normal when Coulter shows up."

"You take care of yourself," she ordered, wagging a finger at Simon. "Your grandfather will skin me alive if I let anything happen to you on my watch."

Simon laughed, warmed by the thought of his efficient but acerbic assistant standing up to Coulter on his behalf. "We're okay, Dora. Nothing's going to happen. They'll serve the warrant, he'll open the box and we'll deal with whatever we have to deal with. I'll call you when I leave."

"Please do," she ordered. Then, darting a glance at Ben, she added, "You make sure he follows through."

"Yes, ma'am," they answered in unison.

Once Dora left, Ben got up to go check on Alicia, Hayes and the agents holed up in Simon's office. Simon tipped his head back and closed his eyes, breathing deeply to calm his agitation. The urge to text Lori and remind her to be careful roiled inside of him, but the notion was ridiculous. Of the two of them, she was far more capable of taking care of herself. He had one guy to face. She would be facing a group of hostile employees scrambling for what to do when presented with a search warrant.

The sound of the outer door opening jolted him from his thoughts. He rose from the conference room chair and stepped into the foyer to greet his client. Coulter looked cool and tousled. He wore a pair of dark pants cut loose and flowing. His shirt was unbuttoned. Simon couldn't help thinking if the man were not handsome, the look would be retro ridiculous.

"Good afternoon," he said, forcing a note of welcome into his voice. "How was the drive down from Atlanta?"

"Drive?" Coulter accepted Simon's hand and gave it a perfunctory shake, offering his slippery smile. "I never said I drove. A friend of mine has a helicopter. I hitched a ride with him."

"Flying beats driving any day." Simon tried for a chuckle, but almost choked on it.

Ben stepped out of Simon's office, followed closely by an officer from the Georgia Department of Natural Resources Law Enforcement Division. They crossed in front of Dora's desk, and Coulter stiffened. He darted a glance at Simon, but otherwise kept his cool. "Sheriff Kinsella, what brings you here?"

Gesturing to the other man, he said, "This is Terrence Scroggins. He's an officer with the Department of Natural Resources. They received information of a parcel being delivered to this address containing a live animal. Officer Scroggins needs to inspect the parcel."

Coulter's eyes narrowed and sharpened. "How did the Department of Natural Resources hear about this particular delivery?"

"We monitor all shipments under the Lacey Act," Officer Scroggins provided helpfully. "We do random inspections when we see an increase in activity."

Coulter did not look amused. "Two shipments is considered an increase in activity? I hope you're not monitoring my Amazon account. You'd be completely overwhelmed."

Scroggins chuckled at the joke. "No, we're more than happy to leave your shopping to you. We're only concerned about parcels containing creatures."

The man smiled and rested his hands on his hips above his utility belt. Simon couldn't help but notice the wildlife officer seemed to carry much the same equipment Ben and Lori did on theirs. He felt a wave of relief at being on the side of the two men in the room who were armed.

"The tracking is done by recipient, not by address," Officer Scroggins informed him. "We track the number of parcels delivered to your own address, Mr. Coulter. I assure you it is simply a matter of numbers."

Simon gestured to the conference room. "Well, shall we?" He waved an arm toward the door. "I'm not sure about the rest of y'all, but I want to get on with my evening. I'm assuming if this is a matter of routine, it shouldn't take long."

They moved into the conference room, and Officer Scroggins produced an impressive array of tools as he inspected the markings on the box carefully. "Of course, I'll need to measure the specimen to make sure it's within proper regulations." He shot them an open, unassuming smile. "You wouldn't believe the things people try to get away with shipping because they think nobody's paying attention."

Simon watched the man place a pair of gloves, some calipers and a tape measure on the credenza beside the box. "Mr. Coulter, if you'd please open your parcel, I'll inspect the specimen and we'll all be on our way."

Coulter hung back, his gaze traveling from the game warden to the sheriff, then to Simon. "What happens if I refuse?"

"Sir, I assure you it's purely routine," Scroggins interjected.

"I'm speaking to my lawyer," Coulter snapped.

Moving slowly, the game warden stepped to the conference table, pulled his cell phone from his belt and held it up for Coulter to see. "A couple of measurements, a few photos, and we should be all good."

Simon leaned in to talk to his client in a low voice. "Go ahead and open it. Get this over with."

"In all my years of collecting snakes, I've never

had an inspection take place after delivery," Coulter said warily. "You'll forgive me if I'm dubious, but my dealings with the Masters County Sheriff's Department so far have not been what I would consider cordial."

Ben pulled an envelope from his back pocket and handed it to Simon. "I will concede your client has a point. You'll find the search warrant in there."

Coulter snorted and cast a derisive look at the envelope. "A search warrant seems extreme for a routine inspection, doesn't it, Sheriff?"

Ben shrugged. "You said it—our relationship hasn't been particularly smooth up to this point. Officer Scroggins asked me if we would have any difficulty gaining your cooperation, and I advised him I had concerns."

Coulter crossed his arms over his chest. "I'm not opening it."

Ben didn't take his eyes off the man. "Simon, you might want to advise your client to comply."

"Yes," Simon said slowly. "It would be in your best interest to go along with what they're asking." He made a show of opening the envelope and withdrawing the search warrant. He could feel Coulter's gaze creeping over him. He scanned the page, pretending to check every dot on the *i*'s and crossbar on the *t*'s. "This seems to be in order."

There was a protracted silence. Then Coulter gestured to the box. "I didn't sign for this parcel."

The simple statement made Simon's blood boil. "No, of course you didn't."

"I'm not opening anything I did not sign for." Coulter placed a hand squarely in the center of Simon's back and propelled him forward. Simon stared down at the box. The label affixed to the box said it all. Boa Constrictor. Adult Female.

"Mr. Wingate signed for this particular parcel. It was delivered to his address and he took receipt of it."

"Again, we tracked the intended recipient," Officer Scroggins said, keeping his tone genial. "It's addressed to you in care of Mr. Wingate."

"Mr. Wingate is my attorney," Coulter snapped.

Harrison Hayes chose that moment to make his appearance. "Afternoon, Mr. Coulter."

Simon glanced back to see Samuel Coulter sneer at the district attorney. A belligerent set to his jaw, Coulter shoved his hands into the pockets of his pleated pants and fixed them with a stubborn glare.

"Well, now it's a party," he drawled.

"I have an invitation." Harry held up a folded piece of paper. "This is an affidavit signed and sworn before Judge Nichols saying Simon Wingate accepted this package on your behalf as you requested."

He moved to thrust the piece of paper at Coulter, but rather than taking it, the man pulled his hands from his pants pockets and grabbed Simon's left arm in a viselike grip. "You set me up?"

In a flash, Coulter had Simon's wrist twisted up behind his back. Simon bit back a yelp of pain as the man added a little extra torque to his hold on him. "What? They just want you to open the box."

"I'll have your license for this," Coulter hissed.

Simon's brain flashed to Lori. She was about to run onto Samuel Coulter's property with a piece of paper, a firearm and her conviction that she'd been right about Coulter all along. He had to make sure this man was neutralized so she could complete her mission.

Simon saw Ben step closer. "Seriously, Coulter, assaulting your attorney isn't going to help the situation."

Coulter urged Simon to take another step toward the box. "I can buy and sell you all six times over. By the time I'm done with you, you won't be able to get a job sweeping floors in any police department, Sheriff." He drew a ragged breath. "And you…" He jerked on Simon's arm again. "You're finished before you even begin. Any thoughts you had of a career beyond this Podunk town are over. I'll have your law license. I'm gonna—"

"Take the damn box," Simon ordered. "Take it and get out of here. We're done."

Coulter let out a hard bark of laughter. "How stupid do you think I am? My fingerprints aren't on the box, but yours are. I bet you have pictures of it too. I can't help it if people put my name on a mailing label. This isn't my address. I'm not the one who's into this up to his neck."

A shot rang out and they all jumped.

Coulter's grip loosened, and seeing his opening, Simon broke his client's hold on him, grasped the other man's wrist and twisted until he heard a crack. The sound both sickened and energized him. Coulter cried out and dropped to one knee, and the sheriff moved in.

"Hold it right there, Coulter." Simon looked up to find Ben standing over them, his service weapon drawn and trained on Coulter.

"You wanna talk assault," Coulter ground out from between clenched teeth. "I'm pressing charges. I think he broke my wrist."

"We'll see who's pressing charges against who after we open this box," Ben said, signaling for the officer from the state department of natural resources to step forward. "Officer Scroggins, if you wouldn't mind?" he said, tilting his head toward the box.

Officer Scroggins stepped around Coulter, his service weapon trained on the man. "I do believe this is the first opportunity I've had to fire my weapon in almost twenty-two years of service. Well, fire it around humans, I mean," he amended. "Had to put down some animals," he explained as he holstered his sidearm. "Sorry I took a chunk out of your side table here."

Dazed, Simon looked over to see a fresh chunk of wood splintered out of the credenza just beneath where the box sat.

Simon shook his head to clear it. "Yeah, uh, no worries." He pushed himself up onto all fours, then rose shakily, gripping the side of the conference table to get his balance. Then he flopped into the nearest chair, feeling almost boneless in the wake of the adrenaline rush. When his gaze met the concerned gaze of the DA, he attempted a smile. He was fairly sure it fell short. "I guess all those tae kwon do classes my parents popped for finally paid off."

Hayes's mouth thinned into a line. He watched Coulter grasping his wrist and gritting his teeth. The man gave up on trying to stand, pain and fury etched into every line on his face. No one made any attempt to help the man, and he finally gave up, twisting around to sit on the floor, grumbling threats and cradling his injured hand. "They certainly did."

Special Agent Simmons and a gentleman from the US Department of the Interior skidded to a halt in the foyer. They peered around Hayes, trying to get a handle on the scene.

"What the hell is going on here?" Simmons demanded.

Feeling light-headed, Simon dropped into the nearest chair and blew out a huff of breath. "He didn't want to open the box." He shifted his gaze to the man on the floor. The second their eyes met, he said, "I resign. In light of this…situation, I can no longer be your attorney."

"I'll ruin you," Coulter ground out between clenched teeth.

Simon remembered the confidence his father and grandfather had in his ability to decide what was best for him. And for them all. "Go ahead. Do whatever you think you can do."

"Mr. Coulter refused to open the parcel. Officer Scroggins has agreed to do so for us," Ben informed the newcomers.

Officer Scroggins unfolded a multipurpose tool

and slit the tape securing the package with brisk efficiency. Simon held his breath as the man lifted the lid and removed foam insulation. A moment later, he reached in and pulled out a loosely coiled snake Simon figured might stretch as long as the conference table. Everyone but Coulter jumped back when he placed the snake on the table.

"Don't worry—she's dead," Scroggins pronounced flatly.

"She might be hibernating," the man from the US Department of the Interior offered.

Officer Scroggins turned a piercing gaze toward Coulter. "But she isn't hibernating, is she, Mr. Coulter."

"I have no idea what's wrong with that snake. I ordered it from a catalog—"

"You ordered it from your friend Ramon Calderon, in Miami," Alicia interjected.

"And your friend Ramon didn't do a very good job with packing her," Scroggins said grimly.

Simon watched in dazed horror as the wildlife officer turned the limp snake over to show a pattern of irregular lumps and bumps pressing against the scaly skin, and a long, sloppily sewed incision mark. Before Simon could get a closer look, Scroggins used the same tool to reopen the incision, and a handful of tied-off condoms filled with powder spilled out onto the table.

Alicia Simmons didn't miss a beat. "Samuel Coulter, I'm Special Agent Alicia Simmons of the Drug Enforcement Administration. You are under arrest…"

Her words faded in and out. Simon couldn't help staring at the gaping wound in the snake. He'd never been one to embrace God's more slippery creatures, but his stomach twisted at the sight of the poor creature split open. Who came up with this madness? What kind of sociopath—

"Mr. Wingate?" the DEA agent called out to him.

"Huh?" Simon jerked his gaze from the snake and forced himself to refocus. "I'm sorry?"

"You no longer represent Mr. Coulter—is that correct?"

"That's correct," he and Coulter replied, nearly in unison. Finally, they agreed on one thing.

"I called for an ambulance," the officer from the US Department of the Interior announced, shoving his phone back into his pocket. "Two of your guys are on their way over to escort Mr. Coulter to the regional medical center for an X-ray."

Ben shoved his weapon back into its holster, then produced a zip tie. "Cuffs might be hard on a crunchy wrist." He offered the long strip of heavy-duty plastic to Alicia. "He doesn't strike me as the type to fight through the pain, but if you want me to secure his good hand to something until the ambulance arrives, I'm sure Simon won't mind."

Alicia nodded. "Good. Thank you." Turning back to Coulter, she smiled as Ben pulled Coulter's good hand from his lap and lashed it to the arm of one of the massive leather boardroom chairs. "Mr. Coulter, at this moment federal agents are serving a warrant to search your property located on Highway 19. We expect to add additional charges pending the search and seizure there."

At the mention of Coulter's compound, Simon shot from his chair and stepped over Coulter's outstretched arm to get to the door. Harrison caught his arm. "Where do you think you're going?"

"Lori—" He swung around and stared imploringly at Ben. "I have to get out there."

"Listen, I know. I'm worried too, but there's an operation underway. We can't go running into the middle of it all. She has a job to do, and she won't thank you for getting in the way."

"I'm not going to get in the way, but I have to be there."

Ben looked over at Alicia, and the agent gave him a shrug and a small smile. "Go on. I'm sure I can keep this slippery guy in my sights until our transport arrives. I'll meet you out there."

THE SHERIFF'S SUV flew down Highway 19 headed away from Pine Bluff and toward Lori. Toward whatever trouble she was facing at Samuel Coulter's godforsaken Reptile Rendezvous. Simon clung to the handle above the door, not because he wanted Ben to slow down, but more because he needed to feel tethered to something.

They were more than halfway there when the sheriff spoke up. "I'm not gonna be all paternal and ask what your intentions are."

When he paused to draw breath, Simon jumped in. "Good."

"Her father is gone," Ben said, holding up a finger to forestall any of Simon's protests. "So I have to ask…am I gonna have to kick your ass for hurting her?"

"Not if I can help it," Simon said gruffly.

It was the truth. He would do anything he could to keep from hurting her. He couldn't think about his own motivations now. All he could focus on was the possibility of someone hurting her while they had a heart-to-heart in the car.

"Can you go any faster?"

Ben gave a grim shake of his head. "I'm already doing thirty over."

Simon sighed. He knew Ben was right to be careful. There wasn't a lot of traffic on the highway, but it was late afternoon, and people who lived in the outlying areas of the county were heading home from work. Each and every car they'd come upon had yielded to the blue lights and sirens, but they could encounter somebody who didn't see or hear them coming.

"We're going to get there, and she's going to be fine," Ben assured him.

"We haven't even talked about what this thing is," Simon said quietly.

Ben leaned in. "What thing?"

"Lori and me. This *thing* between us." He murmured the last part, unable to work the words past the lump rising in his throat. Propping his elbow on the door, he ran his forefinger over his lip, wiping away the fine sheen of perspiration. "I mean, I can't even name it, and she might not—"

"She does," Ben stated flatly. When Simon glanced over at him, the sheriff shrugged. "When you work closely with someone, you get a gut feeling when something's going on with them. She's still grieving, though. Both for her family and for Jeff Masters. It's made her question a lot of her choices. No doubt she's questioning her feelings for you. You'll just have to be patient and let her find her way back to herself. Can you do that?"

"Yes. Yes, I can do that." Ben's plainspoken words were a balm. Simon leaned forward in the seat, the nylon restraint tightening against his chest. "I just… She was right all along. About Coulter. About me. If something happens to her because of Coulter—"

"If something happens to her, it would be because she's doing her job. A job she's damn good at, I might add." The two men shared a glance, and Ben refocused on the road. "She's essentially been a cop since she was nineteen years old. Her job is her life, which is what makes her so good at it."

Ben let up on the accelerator and they cruised up a rise in the road. They crested the hill. Below, flashes of blue light cut through the smoke filling the late-afternoon sky.

"She's going in after the girls, right?"

Ben nodded. "The Feds will handle the search and seizure on any drugs found on the premises. Lori has strict instructions to get in there, check the barracks at the back of the lot to see if there are any young women being held in there and get them out without interfering with the rest of the operation."

"I hate that she's going in there alone," Simon muttered.

Ben ran a hand over his forehead, then spoke gruffly. "I do too. She was going to try to round up Deputy Wasson from Prescott County to see if he'd back her up."

Simon tightened his grip on the handle. "Has anyone heard from her?"

The sheriff shrugged. "She's not going to stop and make a phone call in the middle of an operation."

"What about the radio?" Simon asked, gesturing to the unit mounted into the dash.

"I explained about the police band thing earlier."

"Yeah, but the thing's in motion now. Shouldn't y'all be in communication?"

Simon saw the corner of the sheriff's mouth tighten. It was a tell. Ben was worried too. They should've heard something by now.

The sheriff let up on the gas. "Why are you slowing down?"

"Red lights." He pointed to the rearview mirror, and Simon twisted in his seat. Sure enough, two trucks from the volunteer fire department zoomed past.

"We're never going to get there," Simon complained.

Ben snorted and peeled away from the shoulder with a spray of gravel. "Keep your pants on. I'm not going to let you go in there after her," he pointed out.

"But—"

"No buts. You are a civilian, Counselor. The only reason I brought you on this ride-along is because you'd probably try to hitch a skateboard to my back bumper if I didn't. I need you to stay in the car."

Simon was about to protest, but a sudden crackle of static burst from the radio. He stared at the dashboard, willing it to come to life again.

Ben applied the brakes once more, and this time he hooked a sharp right into the field used as a parking lot. Police and other emergency services vehicles sat parked in a haphazard fashion. Ben pressed the lock button and held it. With his other hand, he cut the engine. "Am I gonna have to put you in the back seat to keep you safe?"

Simon simply stared back at him. "No. I know my place here."

Ben nodded and reached for the door handle. "Sit tight. I'll get you an update as soon as I can."

Simon waited until Ben disappeared into a small knot of people gathered at the side of a black van. The moment the sight line was broken, he opened the car door and slipped out. The flattened grass muffled his footsteps as he headed away from Ben and the other law enforcement types. He had one mission in mind—get to Lori and help however he could.

Chapter Sixteen

Lori signaled to Deputy Steve Wasson of Prescott County to follow her. To his credit, the older man did so without hesitation. When she filled Steve in on the plan to get in and get whatever girls Coulter might have stashed on the property out, the Prescott County deputy had been all for it. The discovery of Kaylin Bowers on Samuel Coulter's property had helped them form a bond over a common enemy.

They'd entered the woods far away from the commotion the federal agents made at the front entrance. Instead, they hopped the fence that ran along the side of the property. Staying low, she wound her way through the trees and scrubby underbrush, following the main footpath but staying off it in case she came across any resistance. Her mission was technically to secure and collect any of Coulter's employees, but she wanted to get to the building undetected first. In case there were people trapped there who might need help.

Bella Nunes had told her she'd stayed in a sort of dormitory at the far end of the grounds, and that other young women were staying there too. Kaylin Bowers's parents claimed their daughter had been tight-lipped and belligerent since her return home, but she had agreed to talk to Lori. Briefly. Kaylin confirmed the existence of such a building and mentioned there were a few other girls staying there at the time she'd been there. She claimed they locked the door from the outside at night to prevent people from wandering the park and to keep the female members of the staff "safe."

Making her way through the wooded area, Lori carefully moved aside branches and pointed out fallen tree trunks to Wasson. Though she had her service weapon holstered at her hip, Lori was more comforted by the rifle in her hand. These woods were her home. This was her backyard.

The path widened beside her, and she slowed her steps. The canopy of leaves and needles trapped the worst of the smoke from the nearby fires. She moved in a crouch. The trunks of the young pines were inadequate cover, but since she was dressed in her tactical gear, someone would have to be looking hard to find her.

When they'd studied the aerial shots of Coulter's property, Lori had been the one to point out the large Quonset hut–style building at the rear of the property. She had to give Special Agent Simmons credit. She didn't bat an eye when Lori told her she wanted to run straight into the remote area of the compound. Nor did the special agent try to stand in her way.

Less than a quarter mile up the fire road, the roof

of the building came into sight. They slowed, creeping toward the low barracks on silent feet. About fifty yards out, still hidden in the cover of the tree line, Lori held up a hand signaling Wasson to stop.

Cupping her hands around her mouth, she shouted, "Masters County Sheriff's Department. Is anyone in there?"

When there was no reply, she faced the other deputy. "I'm gonna need you to circle around to the end and cover the other door, but let me try to get them out on this end. They may respond better to a female voice." Wasson simply nodded. "We need to get into the building without fuss or firepower. Get me?"

"I'm with you."

"If my intel is right, there are likely teenage girls in there. I figure they are unarmed and definitely freaking out. We need to proceed with extreme caution."

"Got you," Wasson replied.

"Radio check," she whispered into her mic. When she heard his clipped response of "Check," they split up.

Moving in a wide circle, Lori approached the door on the far end from behind the hinges. If someone came bursting out, she could use the door as cover. She settled into position against the building's wall. Inspecting the door on their side, she spotted the padlock holding a large metal hasp closed.

"Crud," she muttered. Then she whispered into her mic. "Far door padlocked."

The reply from Wasson came through the earpiece.

"Same." There was a crackle of static. Then he asked, "Shoot it off?"

She scoffed, then keyed the mic. "Negative. That only works in movies." She eyed the padlock, then continued. "Stay put. I'm going to bust it off. No shooting unless someone shoots at us first."

She sprang forward and used the butt end of her rifle to pound the hasp three times in rapid succession. A cacophony of high-pitched screams came from inside the building, and Lori dropped to the ground, waiting to see if anyone inside attempted to fire on her.

From her low vantage point, she could see the screws securing the hasp to the ancient building were giving way, but the lock held.

Then a trembling voice pleaded, "Help us."

Lori sprang to her feet and slammed the stock down on the rusted metal again. On her second blow, one side popped loose. "Hang on," she called to them.

Using her bare hands, she peeled the whole thing back enough to open the door, then stepped aside for cover. "Sheriff's department," she shouted again. "We have the building surrounded. Drop your weapons!"

"We don't have any weapons," a young woman cried. "I swear!"

Lori took a deep breath and swung the door open wide, praying the occupants were telling the truth. Lori squatted low and tipped her head around the edge of the door to sneak a peek.

Three girls who appeared to be in their midteens huddled together on one of the narrow beds at the center of the room, their arms wrapped tightly around one another. Exhaling heavily, Lori let the relief wash over her.

"Come out now. Keep your hands high where we can see them." When the girls failed to move, she barked, "Now!"

They untangled themselves in a flurry of long, coltish limbs. Sobbing and staggering, the girls stumbled toward the door, their hands held high.

"Coming out on my end," she said into the radio.

"Ten-four," came Wasson's reply.

Her breathing returned to something approximating normal when Wasson came trotting around the side of the building, weapon raised and ready.

"They're unarmed," Lori called to him.

"We should secure them," he said, his voice pitched low. "As a precaution. At least until they've cleared all the personnel from the grounds."

The impulse to argue was strong, but the man was right. Until they had these girls processed, there was no way to know if and how they were involved in Coulter's operations. Reluctantly, she and Wasson started to zip-tie the sobbing girls' wrists to one another, all the while trying to reassure them that they were just being careful.

"What the hell are you doing?"

The breathless demand shot up Lori's spine. Wasson pivoted in the blink of an eye, his sidearm unholstered and aimed directly at Simon Wingate.

Lori exhaled in a whoosh, then placed a calming

hand on the deputy's arm. "Ease up. He's one of the good guys."

At least, she thought he was.

He stood there with his arms raised in surrender. She saw his suit jacket was torn at the shoulder, his matching pin-striped pants were covered in dust and grime, and his polished shoes were caked with mud and leaves.

"I'm going to turn that question back on you, Counselor. What do you think you're doing here?"

"Helping you," he replied, still a little out of breath but unapologetic. "I thought you came up here alone."

Lori shook her head, then gestured to the man beside her. "Deputy Steve Wasson, Prescott County, meet Samuel Coulter's attorney, Simon Wingate."

"Former attorney," Simon corrected quickly. "Samuel Coulter's former attorney."

"They have him in custody?" They wouldn't have gotten the go-ahead on the compound if they didn't, so it was more a statement than a question, but Lori craved the eyewitness confirmation. Particularly from this particular witness.

"Yes. He's in custody." Simon flashed her a shaky but reassuring smile. "But why are you cuffing these young ladies? They haven't done anything wrong, have they?"

"That's yet to be determined," Deputy Wasson replied. "But we don't believe so," he added, raising his voice to be heard over the fresh round of sobs rising around him.

"We're just securing them until we can be sure

everything has gone off as expected." She craned her neck and looked up at the fog of smoke trapped in the treetops. "What's on fire?"

Simon shrugged. "From what I can gather, random structures."

"Literally a smoke screen," Lori murmured. Glancing over her shoulder at the three girls strapped hand to hand, she gave them as reassuring a smile as she could muster. "Deputy Wasson is going to take you down to base via the fire lane," she told them. "There will be officers there to take your statements." She picked up the rifle she'd set against the building. "Mr. Wingate will go with you. He's an attorney, and no doubt looking for some new clients."

"Hey," Simon objected.

She heard the injury in his tone and softened a little. "A joke," she said, raising a hand.

"Where are you going?" he asked as she shooed them away.

"I'm going back through the woods. I want to make sure none of Coulter's guys go slithering off under cover of smoke."

"But—"

Ignoring the fleeting impulse to hurl herself at him and thank him for caring enough to come after her, she lifted her rifle into ready position, then jerked her chin toward Wasson. "But nothing. Go with him."

"Lori, I—"

"Simon, I appreciate your concern, but this is what I am trained for. This is what I do. And I can't do what

I need to do and cover you too. Go. We'll talk when I get down there."

To her relief, he clamped his mouth shut, took the arm of the girl closest to him, and they started walking from the far end of the Quonset hut to the dirt road beyond the tree line. Lori watched until they were out of sight, then pulled her own disappearing act.

The woods were eerily quiet. There was no birdsong or chirruping of insects. No doubt the smoke from the fires and commotion down below had sent all the wildlife to ground. Which meant the only creatures stirring in these woods would be up to no good.

The trail she'd been following spilled into a single-lane gravel road. She crept closer, crouching low and scanning the length of the road until she spotted a prefabricated building near where the road intersected with the fire lane.

Lori frowned, trying to recall whether she'd seen the road on the aerial photographs the DEA had provided. Probably not. A car was backed up to the door. The late-afternoon sun blazed off the windshield. Lifting her rifle, she peered through the scope for a better look. It was a dull gray Toyota, more primer than paint, with a large wing attached to its open trunk. This was Rick Dale's car. Seeing the ridiculous spoiler attached to the compact car made her think of Simon.

"Wasson, hold up," she whispered into the mic. "Take cover for a minute."

A second later, the reply came. "Ten-four."

Raising the rifle, she used the scope to scan the

area. The car was backed in close to the building. The rear bumper nearly touched the door. A light shone from the inside, slicing out into the smoky haze settling over the area. She hunched down and watched. A thin, tattooed man in a black concert T-shirt carried two duffel bags from the building and deposited them into the open trunk.

Opening her mic, she called for the special agent heading up the ground operations. "Ruggalo?" she whispered into her mic.

Special Agent Mark Ruggalo, a man nicknamed Hulk and who could have been used for a recruiting poster, answered. "I read you."

"Do you have eyes on Rick Dale?"

A second later, his gruff "Negative" came through her earpiece.

"I do."

"What's your twenty?"

"There's a metal building on the fire lane that runs the east side of the property. Closer to the rear than front."

"Stick a pin in him if he moves. We're coming."

Lori watched as the guy disappeared back into the building. Then she lowered the muzzle of her rifle. She keyed the switch on her radio again. "Wasson, hold your cover. I'm going to take out his tires, try to slow him down."

Without waiting for any response, she aimed her rifle at the left front tire and put a bullet clean through the sidewall. If Dale heard the crack of her rifle, it didn't deter him from his mission. He appeared again, seemingly oblivious to the deflating tire. She watched him load two more bags into the trunk, then hustle back into the building. Shifting her position, she took aim at the other front tire and put a bullet-sized hole in it too.

Opening her mic, she said, "Flat front tires should hobble him, but you'll want backup, Ruggalo. He's loading something out of here, and I'm betting it's what you're hunting."

The monitor in her ear hissed and crackled. "Ten-four. Almost there," Ruggalo replied.

Lori held her breath, watching Dale's every move and hoping she didn't have to take a shot at him, as well. She'd do it if she had to, but she much preferred not to.

A rustle in the leaves behind her alerted her to someone's approach. Rolling to her side, she drew her sidearm in case there was a close-range confrontation. She'd barely had a chance to aim when Simon Wingate dropped onto the leafy mulch beside her.

"What are you doing? I almost shot you," she hissed.

"Wasson and the girls are hunkered down right over there." He pointed slightly up the slope and to the east. "I saw the sun glint off your scope when you were calling things in."

"Simon, this isn't a game of backyard cops and robbers. I'm not toting a water gun here," she said, exasperated.

He raised both brows, affronted. "I'm aware of that." He scooted his elbows under his chest and lifted his head. "I thought you would like to know that Cassidy—that's one of the girls you rescued—says that's where they keep the 'superexpensive and rare' snakes," he said, squinching to approximate the use of air quotes. "She says only Coulter and his main man have keys."

"Looks like Dale is his main man," she said. Sighing, she set her handgun down in the space between her and Simon and took up her rifle again. Sighting on the door, she growled. "Keep your head down."

She heard a twig crack somewhere off to her left, swung the gun around and blew out a breath of relief when she spotted Ruggalo and his team approaching. Opening her mic, she whispered, "I see you. I'm at two o'clock. Deputy Wasson and the girls from the Quonset hut are somewhere between your three and four. He's loading up, but I don't know how much more that tiny trunk can hold."

Ahead of her, Ruggalo's team moved into position, using hand signals to fan out and surround the building. "What have we got?"

Lori raised her scope and scanned the area and the building. The door stood ajar, but Dale had not reappeared with any more bags. "So far, I've witnessed him placing four large black duffel bags into the trunk of the car. I have no idea what they contain. He's inside."

Ruggalo held up an okay signal to let her know he'd heard her.

"I believe there's only one way in or out. I'll cover your six."

As Ruggalo and his team advanced on the small building, she turned to Simon. He was so close she could feel the moist heat of his breath on her lips. "I'm moving down behind them. I will stay back, but I need you to promise to stay here."

She waited for an argument. After all, the man was a lawyer. She couldn't expect anything different from him, could she? But rather than speaking, he leaned in and pressed his mouth to hers.

Instead of tasting of desperation, fear or impatience, his kiss was soft and sweet. A promise of things to come rather than a last-ditch effort.

When they parted, he pressed his dirt-streaked forehead to her cheekbone near the nylon strap of her tactical helmet and whispered, "Go get 'em."

Her lips still tingling from his kiss, Lori skittered down a slight incline and took up a position well behind the team of federal agents. She settled in, her gun sighted on the open doorway as the men scoped the area and conveyed information to one another using the tactical gestures she knew as well as she knew the alphabet.

Ruggalo dispatched his men with swift efficiency. She wrapped her finger around the trigger as the agent nearest to the door shouted their identification and warned the occupant that they had the building surrounded.

Thankfully, Rick Dale seemed to have a well-developed sense of self-preservation. Or he knew damn good and well he wasn't the one who would bear the brunt of whatever the Feds were about to rain down on Samuel Coulter. That was the thing with drug busts. There was usually someone higher up in the food chain to squeal on.

After a tense minute, they heard the man inside the building call out, "Don't shoot. Okay?"

He came out of the building with his hands held above his head. They instructed him to stand facing the side of the shed, his hands pressed high on the wall. One agent held him at gunpoint and barked questions while another patted him down. Dale claimed he was alone. Within minutes, they had confirmed his story and cleared the area. The Toyota's trunk and doors stood wide open.

Ruggalo stood up from his position between Lori and the rest of his team. "What's in the bags?"

Dale simply shook his head. "I'm not talking until I get a lawyer, but I wouldn't open them if I was you, man."

For a split second, Lori was afraid Simon would jump up out of the leaf mulch and volunteer his services, but to her immense relief, he held his silence.

One of the agents walked over to the trunk and nudged one of the duffel bags with the barrel of his gun. Lori stared through the scope, her stomach roiling as she watched the bag undulate.

She pressed the button on her mic and said to Ruggalo, "Snakes. No telling what else he has in there, but he definitely has snakes."

"Ten-four," Ruggalo called back.

Three more agents trotted into the clearing. They wore windbreakers rather than the full tactical gear the others had, but they were carrying assault weapons. Ruggalo waved them over to the building. Lori rose to her knees as Ruggalo called their progress to the base. He was just nodding at Alicia Simmons's response of "Ten-four. Return to base" when the crack of rifle fire made them jump.

Lori watched in horror as Ruggalo stumbled backward and fell to the ground. But then her entire world squeezed down to a pinpoint. Falling back to her belly, she marked the agent's position and calculated possible trajectories. Lori instinctively swung her rifle into position, using the scope to scan the woods to her left.

She saw the glint of another scope and fired on instinct.

Her weapon's report seemed to echo back at her. She heard the telltale thud of a body landing hard on the soft forest floor and exhaled in a whoosh. She pushed up and rocked back onto her knees. Using the scope, she found a thin young man stretched out prone on a bed of pine needles and crunchy leaves.

Behind her, Simon bellowed her name. She turned to find him running toward her, her own service weapon extended in front of him. The moment he was within reach, she grabbed a handful of his suit coat and yanked him down beside her.

"What do you think you're doing?" She snatched her gun from his grasp. "Do you even know anything about guns?"

"I don't need to," he said, panting. "You do."

"Well, the first thing you need to know is that a handgun isn't going to do you any good at long range," she said, checking the weapon. Thankfully, he hadn't been foolish enough to discharge it.

"I'd do it, though. I'd do it to protect you," he said fervently.

"It's a good thing I don't need protecting," she shot back.

She tore her eyes off the handsome idiot beside her as she spotted two of the backup team sprinting across to check on the shooter. To her relief, she saw Ruggalo work himself up onto one elbow. She watched as the agent probed the front of the Kevlar vest that had saved his life.

"You okay?" Lori asked into the radio.

"Yeah. Knocked the wind out of me," he responded weakly. "Good shootin', Deputy. You're an ace."

Glancing over at her ragtag group covered in the dust of the day, she keyed her mic and said, "Base, this is Cabrera. We had a situation, but the threat has been neutralized. Send medical and backup."

THE SCENE IN the parking lot had grown exponentially in the time since he'd slipped out of Ben Kinsella's SUV. Simon knew there'd be hell to pay for that, but he was too busy getting an earful from the diminutive deputy walking down the dirt track beside him to care.

"Wow. Look at this," he said, gesturing to the carnival of flashing lights atop nearly every vehicle.

While they were in the woods, a command center had popped up. Almost every foot of the field was covered with emergency vehicles. He noted at least three counties other than Masters present. Then there were the black panel vans and unmarked cars used by the Feds. His hands shook with unspent adrenaline.

Personnel scurried from group to group. Firemen in full turnout gear clumped back and forth and up and down trails shouting instructions to one another. Lori raised a hand to Deputy Wasson as he herded the three young women they found toward a black van parked beside an ambulance.

Special Agent Ruggalo sat in the open back door of an ambulance, medics crawling all over him as he spoke into a mobile phone. Lori raised her hand in a wave and he responded with a salute and a thumbs-up.

Simon spotted Ben Kinsella standing with the sheriff from Prescott County, their heads bent together in conversation. "Guess I'd better go let Ben get his shots in on me."

Lori grabbed his arm and spun him around to face her beside a Prescott County cruiser. "That was probably the most harebrained thing a person could possibly do. What were you thinking?" she demanded.

"I was thinking I needed to get to you." He waved an all-encompassing hand at the scene around them. "I knew your mission was not the DEA's mission. I didn't know if you had backup and I couldn't let you run off into the woods alone."

"Stop there," she advised. "Simon, I was doing my job."

"I know—"

"A job I've had since I was nineteen. A job I'm damn good at doing."

"I know you are. But I was worried sick. What if you went in there and I never got a chance to tell you—"

He stopped abruptly and took a moment to search her eyes. "Give me… I just need to…" He stopped, then gripped her upper arms gently and turned her away from him.

"What are you doing?" she demanded.

He found the catch for her chin strap and popped it open. Lifting the helmet from her head, he sighed when he caught sight of the thick, heavy knot of hair coiled at her nape. Ducking his head, he pressed his lips to the spot he'd ached to kiss since the moment he first laid eyes on her. Her skin was damp and dusty, but he didn't care. She was alive and warm and everything he needed.

"I have been aching to do this." She shivered and he pressed another gentle kiss to the sensitive spot. "The first time I saw you, all I could do was think about kissing you right here," he whispered. "Taking your hair down. Sliding my fingers through it."

"Simon—"

"I know this isn't the time or place, but, Lori, I need you to know I am not sorry I went in after you. I'd have done anything I needed to do to save you, because I am on your side, Lori. I want to be by your side.

"And, logically, yes, I know what I did today was boneheaded." He chuckled and squeezed her arms tight as he pressed his cheek to her hair. "But logic doesn't work when it comes to how I feel about you."

He felt the breath rush out of her and gathered her close, pulling her back against him. "You were right about me at the start. I wasn't giving Pine Bluff a chance," he said with a wry smile. "I didn't plan on staying here one minute longer than I had to."

She stiffened. "And now?"

Drawing a bracing breath, he loosened his hold and urged her to turn to face him. "To be honest, I've never sat down and thought long and hard about what I want to do or where I want to be." He blew out a breath. "I took the path laid out in front of me the minute I was born."

"It's what most of us do."

"Not you," he countered.

Lori wet her lips. "Not me."

"All my life, I've been trying to find shortcuts. Why bother paying dues or taking time to think about whether I might actually want something different, right?"

"Right," she whispered.

"I was wrong," he said, holding her gaze. "I was so wrong. I had no idea everything I ever wanted might be right here."

"Simon—"

"Listen, this is new. You and me. And I told Ben, I'm not even sure you actually think it's a thing, but… My parents are so in love with each other," he whispered, looking straight into her eyes. "I'm supposed to want all the other stuff. The power, ambition, adulation, but in truth, all I ever wanted was someone who simply wanted me. Was happy with me just the way I am."

She swallowed the lump in her throat. "I get you."

"I haven't done anything to make you believe in me, but I—"

"I haven't been nice to you," she interrupted. "I haven't given you much of a chance, and I'm sorry."

He gave her a lopsided smile. "You've been a challenge. And believe it or not, I don't mind a challenge."

"I guess we're a better match than I thought," she said with a laugh.

"We are," Simon replied, but he wasn't laughing. "You challenge me, Lori, and in doing so, you make me think about what I want to accomplish. Who I want to be. And I think I'm starting to figure it out."

"Are you?"

"Yes."

"And who do you want to be?"

"I want to be the guy who gets to kiss you. More than that, I want to be the guy who *deserves* to kiss you."

Lori licked her lips, pressed the heels of her hands to the corners of her eyes and stomped her booted foot as she looked away from him. "Don't make me cry. I'm in uniform," she said in a low rush.

Simon's smile came slowly, but when it ramped up to full strength, it was dazzling. "Well, I certainly don't want to make you cry out of uniform."

"Cocky," she admonished, her voice husky with emotion.

"Hopeful," he corrected. "Hopeful you'll give me

a chance. Hopeful you'll show me how good small-town life can be."

She whipped her head up and her gaze met his. "You're staying here?"

"I think so," he said, the idea solidifying in his mind. "Something about this place feels like home. And don't think it doesn't pain me to admit it."

"I know it does," she said, a smile tugging at her lips.

"Speaking of pain, did I tell you I took Coulter down in more ways than one?"

"Did you? How's that?"

"Turns out I've retained some pretty slick martial arts skills. Remind me to show you my moves later."

She tugged his head down and her smile blossomed as his lips grazed hers. "Oh, I will, Counselor. I definitely will."

* * * * *

"What happens next?" Naomi had an awful, awful feeling that
this was not going away anytime soon.

There were parts of no less than three people out there—of
course it wasn't going away quickly.

"I've put in a call to the FBI office in Nashville. They're going to
send a team to have a look around. Their crime scene investigators
have far more experience and far more state-of-the-art equipment.
If there's anything to be found, they'll find it."

The FBI.

The ability to breathe escaped her for a moment.

The sheriff held up a hand. "Don't get unnerved by the federal
authority becoming involved. I know the agent they're sending,
Casey Duncan. He's a good guy and he knows his stuff. The case
will be in good hands with him."

"But why the FBI? Why not the Tennessee Bureau of
Investigations?" Seemed far more logical to her, but then she knew
little about police work beyond what she saw on television shows
and in movies.

"Considering we have three victims," he explained, "there's a
possibility we're looking at a repeat offender."

He didn't say the words, but she knew what he meant. Serial
killer.

The queasiness returned with a second wind. "Serial killer?"

He gave a noncommittal nod. "Possibly. This is nothing we want going public, but we have to consider all possibilities. Whatever happened here, it happened more than once to more than one person."

She managed to swallow back the bile rising in her throat. "Should I be concerned for my safety?"

"I can't say for sure at this stage, but I'd feel better assigning a security detail. Just as a precaution."

She nodded, the movement so stiff she felt her neck would snap if she so much as tilted her head.

"We've focused our attention on the building where the remains were discovered and the immediate area surrounding it. The FBI will want to search your home. Your office. Basically, everything on the property. It would be best for all concerned if you agreed to all their requests. A warrant would be easy to obtain under the circumstances."

"Of course. Whatever they need to do." She had no reason not to cooperate. No reason at all.

"Good. I'll pass that along to Duncan."

Duncan. The name sounded familiar, but she couldn't place it. "He'll be here today?"

"He will. Might be three or four later this afternoon or early evening, but he will be here today."

"Thank you."

The sooner they figured out what in the world had happened, the sooner life could get back to normal.

She pushed away the idea that normal might just be wishful thinking.

How did a person move on from something like this?

They were talking about murder.

Don't miss
The Bone Room,
available October 2021 wherever
Harlequin Intrigue books and ebooks are sold.

Harlequin.com

Get 4 FREE REWARDS!

We'll send you 2 FREE Books plus 2 FREE Mystery Gifts.

Harlequin Intrigue books are action-packed stories that will keep you on the edge of your seat. Solve the crime and deliver justice at all costs.

FREE Value Over $20

YES! Please send me 2 FREE Harlequin Intrigue novels and my 2 FREE gifts (gifts are worth about $10 retail). After receiving them, if I don't wish to receive any more books, I can return the shipping statement marked "cancel." If I don't cancel, I will receive 6 brand-new novels every month and be billed just $4.99 each for the regular-print edition or $5.99 each for the larger-print edition in the U.S., or $5.74 each for the regular-print edition or $6.49 each for the larger-print edition in Canada. That's a savings of at least 12% off the cover price! It's quite a bargain! Shipping and handling is just 50¢ per book in the U.S. and $1.25 per book in Canada.* I understand that accepting the 2 free books and gifts places me under no obligation to buy anything. I can always return a shipment and cancel at any time. The free books and gifts are mine to keep no matter what I decide.

Choose one: ☐ **Harlequin Intrigue Regular-Print** (182/382 HDN GNXC)   ☐ **Harlequin Intrigue Larger-Print** (199/399 HDN GNXC)

Name (please print)

Address   Apt. #

City   State/Province   Zip/Postal Code

Email: Please check this box ☐ if you would like to receive newsletters and promotional emails from Harlequin Enterprises ULC and its affiliates. You can unsubscribe anytime.

Mail to the **Harlequin Reader Service:**
IN U.S.A.: P.O. Box 1341, Buffalo, NY 14240-8531
IN CANADA: P.O. Box 603, Fort Erie, Ontario L2A 5X3

Want to try 2 free books from another series? Call 1-800-873-8635 or visit www.ReaderService.com.
